GHOST

J.M. DABNEY

EXECUTIONERS BOOK 1

CONTENTS

Dedication

To all my readers who embraced Harper and wanted to know more about her, understood that she needed her happily ever after.

A special thanks to my amazing Beta Readers Tracey, Meredith, Colleen, and Ash. They made this story great.

Author's Note

This book contains scenes of domestic abuse, rape, and mentions of suicide and self-harm. Although, the rape is implied it is clear in the story about what happened.

1 The Pain was All Harper Knew

Her reflection knew all her secrets—most of them weren't pretty. Haunted eyes the shade of bright green stared back at her from the mirror. They were filled more often with tears than she wanted to admit. Harper Sage lived her life under the darkness of her desperation, and no one knew but her. She tilted her head down, her gaze and fingertips stroked the thick crisscrossed scars on one wrist, then the other.

The newest scars were almost a year old. She still remembered the sting of the razor as it sliced easily through the thin, tender flesh. Warm water had turned pink as her heartbeat had steadily pumped the blood from her body. Harper had laid there, she'd grown tired, and her eyes had fluttered shut. Instead of the fear of death, Harper had only felt peace. The self-hate she'd felt for most of her life had washed away as waves ebbing back into the sea.

Harper had thought her struggle was over until she'd awakened to a popcorn ceiling and the steady beat of a heart monitor. Her best friend, Kyle, and his wife were asleep in chairs beside her bed. Her sorrow that the peace she'd experienced was gone had choked her with a macabre sense of failure.

Shaking those thoughts off, she sucked her lips between her teeth and forced back the sobs. Harper put her wide leather cuffs around her wrists to hide most of the scars. Standing up, the long flowing dress fell to her ankles, and the wide sleeves fell to conceal the fingertip bruises on her arms. Harper no longer hurt herself, but she found someone to take care of her self-destruction.

It was time to put on the brave and cheerful face. The one she used to hide the pain of disdain she felt in her hometown. She bent and glanced quickly into the mirror of her vanity to check her makeup before she headed for her bedroom door.

After she'd grabbed her purse, keys and phone, she exited her apartment. She stepped out onto the sidewalk and headed for work as if she were normal. Even though she was anything but.

She turned left and walked passed all the funky little shops on Powers, Georgia's side streets. Main Street looked like any other picturesque small-town scene. The diner, the hardware and farm supply store, salon, barber shop, even a tattoo shop, Twirled World Ink, and to be honest, it was all rather perfect.

Born and raised there, everyone knew everyone else, and everyone's dirty laundry somehow made it to the ears of all. Although Harper was adept at keeping her business to herself, there were some secrets that she couldn't keep from the masses.

Nightingale Books and Cafe was her place of employment, had been since she was sixteen. A mere ten-minute walk from home.

She worked noon to close, but around there that normally meant no later than eight. Harper opened the door and smiled at the tinkling of the old-fashioned bell.

"Oh, Harper, I'm so glad you're here." Her elderly boss Clora Devinne ran as fast as a woman half her age. The woman's exuberance was addictive.

"And why is that? Is Old Man McEnroe trying to seduce you again?" Harper stepped behind the counter and stowed her purse underneath it.

"That old lech wishes he could have me. No, did you hear how our local hermit resident is starting to make an appearance?"

"No, someone actually wants to be seen in this town," she asked sarcastically.

"This is a great town. I hear he's rather handsome."

"Looking for your fifth husband, I see." She leaned her hip against the counter and crossed her arms over her stomach.

"You know no man can handle me. I'm seriously thinking about finding myself a nice girlfriend."

"Switching it up, I hear variety is the spice of life."

"Wouldn't be the first time."

She needed to change the subject quickly. "And with that, why are you so excited about the supposedly handsome, hermit resident?"

"Well, you're young and single."

Oh, she knew where this was going, and she wanted to avoid it as much as a Clora play-by-play of Clora's newest or prospective lover.

"No, I'm quite happy being single." She'd become accustomed to the lie, well not exactly a lie. Harper was some man's secret. He fucked her as long as his Neanderthal friends never found out he spent nights with the transgender freak in town. She'd grown up there, everyone knew from the day she'd worn her first dress in public. Bill had threatened to kill her more than once if anyone found out—she had the bruises to attest to his temper.

"No, you're not,"

Harper didn't bother arguing because she knew it would do her no good. Sometimes matchmaking was Clora's part-time job.

"What sensible woman would want to deal with the backward yokels around here?"

"They're not all that bad."

"Can we change the subject?"

"Fine, the guy is named—"

Harper groaned and strode from behind the counter to the cart of books ready to shelve.

"Don't do that, you know you're curious. I hear he's in King's band."

"No, I'm really not interested, and if he's in King's band, the man is more than likely gay." She had one violent asshole that wouldn't acknowledge her, and she didn't need another. The one she had was plenty to enable her self-destruction and her masochistic borders only extended so far.

"You're no fun, honey,"

"That I won't deny." She moved down each aisle, placed the books and continued all the while Clora dogged her steps.

"You can't spend all your time with Kyle or here. When is the last time you went out?"

She spun toward Clora and the woman merely smiled. "I'm just not sociable."

"Not everyone cares, Harper, and you know that."

"I have proof to the contrary." Surprisingly strong arms wrapped around her and hugged her tight. She blinked rapidly to chase away the tears. Harper smiled as Clora stepped back.

"I'm going to go, community dinner at Bohemia tonight. You should come out to the farm soon, it's been awhile."

"Yeah, Buddha called me the other day to check on me. He's such a pain in the ass." The middle-aged man probably had a last name, yet no one ever asked. He had a small farm outside town. A little Bohemian paradise—a safe haven. In her teens, she's spent more time there than she did at home.

"Yes, he is, but he considers you part of the community, and you know he likes to keep his odd little flock close."

"I told him I'd come out Sunday for Rochelle's Handfasting. She finally found the woman of her dreams."

"Love seems to be in the air out there. Be good, close up early if we don't have anyone after seven."

"Okay."

She loved Clora, but the woman sometimes drove her nuts with the *you need to find a boyfriend* spiel. When the phone rang, she jogged toward the counter and picked up the receiver. "Nightingale Books, how can I help you?"

"Yes, I was wondering what your hours were?"

The gravelly voice was strangely attractive, and the thought took her by surprise.

"The sign says eight, but if we're not busy, we sometimes close at seven."

There was a long pause, and she was about to ask was he still there when he finally spoke. "Okay, thank you."

"You're welcome." She hung up and went to finish the books.

Hours passed slowly with sporadic customers, but Monday was normally a dead day anyway. She curled up on one of the couches with a book and a cup of tea. Clora had said to close up at seven, but she wasn't ready to go home. A bit of reading then she'd get the paperwork done, lock up and then make the night drop.

Harper heard the door open just as she turned the page and she looked up to find a ginger stranger looking around. He was bulky, but not like a bodybuilder, more like someone who worked hard. Yet his belly was rounded giving him a certain softness. His jaw was broad with a full beard and mustache, and he had surprisingly full lips and high cheekbones. His eyes were almond shaped, and they were an odd mix of pale azure and moss green. The stranger's clothes were in good condition, but slightly dirty as were his black work boots.

"Hi, can I help you," she asked as she set her book aside and stood.

"Yeah, I called earlier."

Wow, the voice was sexier in person.

"I'm Harper."

"Gideon. I was told there was a bookstore in town, but I don't come to town much outside of errands."

"For a small store, we have a great selection, but if there's something you want that we don't have, we'll do special orders. You looking for something in particular?"

"I like mysteries and thrillers."

"Heard of O'Brien Shaw?"

"No."

"You're in for a treat, come on, he has a great series. We have most of them, so if you like the first one, we can set you up with the rest." Harper's fingers stroked along the spines. She knew the layout by heart and found what she was looking for easily.

"What kind of books are they?"

"Fifties Noir detective. Very gritty. Damaged hero, but I always find those the most interesting. His writing style is unique. Here." She slipped it from the shelf and handed it to him, Gideon seemed to avoid touching her.

He turned the book over in his hands, and she waited while he read the back.

"Would you like coffee or tea, we have some pastries, cookies."

"No, thank you. Do I have time to look around?"

"We're open until eight."

"But you said you closed at seven, I don't want to keep you."

"It's fine. Take your time and when you're ready I'll be up front."

"Thank you," he whispered and turned his attention back to the book.

She nodded and backed up a few steps, she took the long way to avoid squeezing through the small space between his big body and the shelf.

The shrill ring of the phone caused her to jump, and she rushed to answer it.

"Nightingale Books, how can I help you?"

"I'm coming over." Bill's voice made her cringe.

"I won't be home for a while."

"You should be closed by now."

She could hear the impatience in his voice that didn't bode well for her. The guys he worked with shouted in the background. Some of the voices she heard were slurred and just meant her night would get so much worse.

"I have a customer."

"I'll be at your place in fifteen, get rid of 'em."

"I can't kick him out. I'll be home after he's done and I finish the paperwork."

"Fifteen minutes." The called ended.

Harper held the receiver to her ear as she nervously chewed on her bottom lip. Her hands shook as she hung up. To keep her mind from the pain in store for her when she got home, she started cleaning and getting ready to close. Time passed, and she was turning the open sign off.

"I'm done."

She jumped as Gideon spoke.

"I'm sorry."

"It's fine, my mind was elsewhere. Did you find everything you were looking for?" She turned to find him awkwardly holding an armful of books.

"Yes," he answered and turned toward the checkout counter.

Harper walked behind it and started ringing him up, smiling to herself at some of his choices. She hadn't taken him for the philosophy type, but there were several books by Sartre, Nietzsche and Schopenhauer. She packed them into reusable bags that they used instead of paper or plastic.

"Are the bags extra?"

"No, we don't use anything else. Repeat customers just bring their bags with them. Clora, she owns the place, is very environmentally conscious." She gave him the total, and he handed over his card.

While he signed the slip, she placed several cookies into a paper bag and packed them into one of the bags.

"How much," he asked.

"On the house." He just nodded. "Have a good night."

"You too. It was nice meeting you."

Gideon picked up the bags and headed for the door, she noticed he darted one last look at her before opening the door. Harper wondered what the stranger thought or if he'd heard all the rumors, and she was just the town spectacle.

She watched him until he disappeared from sight and her shoulders drooped, she collapsed into herself. As quickly as possible, she counted the register and ran the credit cards. It didn't take long to write out the deposit. On autopilot, she finished and locked up for the night.

The bank was just across the street, so she put the bag in the night drop and turned to head home. Harper kept a slow pace. She couldn't call Bill her boyfriend, friends with benefits wasn't right either. He was like the slice of a razor, the one she no longer used on the inside of her thighs or wrists. He was the cigarette burns on her stomach. Yet like those things, she didn't want them, but the part of herself that still hated what she used to be, craved them.

She paused at her door, placed her palm on it and closed her eyes. Harper opened it and stepped inside.

"About fucking time. Didn't I tell you fifteen minutes?" Bill kept his voice low, but the backhand to her cheek was loud enough.

Stars exploded behind her closed lids, and her ears rang.

She stumbled backward into the door. His fingers enclosed her throat, and he increased the pressure slowly to draw out her fear. She clawed at his wrist as she struggled to breathe.

"You do what I say, who else would want you, freak." It wasn't a question.

No one else did, or have, and no one else ever would.

Her visions fogged at the corners, the ripping of fabric highlighted his intent. She quickly found herself bent over the couch, there was no kiss or gentle preparation only grunts and searing pain. Each time more violent and painful than the last, but how long did she have to wait for him to do what she couldn't—how long did she have to wait to die?

2 A Ghost in the House

The deep bass of the drum beat vibrated beneath the thick soles of his work boots as it came from the speakers in every corner of the open room. Gideon Jane lifted his perspiring mug to his mouth at regular intervals while he studied the crowd at Brawlers.

His cousin Gregory was wrapped around his husband Bull on the opposite side of the room. Gregory was gorgeous like a model and Bull, twenty years older, with his black hair more silver and his rough edges, perfectly complemented Gregory. They strangely fit and to be honest, he was pathetic by the jealousy he felt over the obvious love Bull had for Gregory. He'd thought he'd had that.

The last few years were filled with too many downs. His twenty-yearlong partnership to the person of his dreams ended. The man he'd thought he'd spend the rest of his life with moved on quickly.

It started out as an awkward blind date in college. Gideon's first with a man. He'd realized he was bisexual in his teens, but with his family, he'd kept it to himself. Once he was away at college, he wouldn't hide anymore. Joe was handsome, a few years older, charming, and funny. The kiss which ended that date was perfect. A year later, they were living together.

Gideon wasn't a small man. Always oversized and too padded around his abdomen, but Joe hadn't minded. Seemed to love the chubby ginger eighteen-year-old. They'd spent hours holding each other; cuddling on the couch or in bed. Or at least that's what he'd believed.

It started out with a perpetual diet, gym memberships, and endless comments about his weight. He wanted to think it was out of love and he'd let himself believe it for years until the first affair he'd forgiven; along with the ones that followed. Men who were lean and handsome, women that were willowy and gorgeous.

The last one he couldn't ignore or forgive because Joe moved out. Gideon felt like an idiot, and that's why he was hiding away on a farm in the middle of nowhere Georgia. The peacefulness after decades living in New York City was just what he had needed.

Powers, Georgia was Gregory's suggestion. And it had been his best decision yet. He had his organic farm, his band The Executioners which he'd joined not long after he'd moved there, and he had family and friends.

Gregory's mom, his aunt, was great. She'd accepted Gregory as gay like it was no big deal.

"Checking out something sexy, Ghost?"

He rolled his eyes at the tiny bartender named Twitch.

Twitch's husband was Crave the head of Brawlers Security. He still couldn't see the blond behemoth and the petite brunet as a couple, but you couldn't mistake the love between them.

"No, not looking for a hookup for the night."

"You've been coming to Brawlers for almost two years, someone must have caught your attention."

"No, leave it alone," he lied.

"Fine, be all grumpy." Twitch huffed and took off to the other end of the bar.

Ghost chuckled and shook his head. He pulled out his wallet and threw some money on the bar and headed home.

###

A book laid open on his thigh as Gideon stared off in the distance and tried to get his chaotic thoughts under control. Gideon's phone ringing pulled him from thoughts he didn't need to think about. He grabbed it and connected the call.

"Are you ready to come home yet?"

His business partner whined into the phone without waiting for his reply.

"No, I left you in charge."

"Yeah, but I can't stand smiling at those catty bitches when I lie to them about being able to make all their stupid impossible dreams come true. If I have to deal with one more wedding, I'm going to start drinking again. It will be your fault if I ruin three years of sobriety."

"Carol, you've threatened that how many times in the last few years?"

"It's still true. Couldn't you have stayed here?"

"No, I couldn't."

"Fine, so how's country living? Any hot country boys or girls catching your fancy?"

"No."

"You said that way too quickly."

He couldn't count the stories he'd heard about Harper since he'd moved there. They hadn't mentioned how beautiful she was, though. He hadn't known what to say, and he probably acted like an idiot. Not his worst first impression but decidedly the one that bugged him.

"Her name is Harper. She works at a local bookstore."

"And?"

"There's no chance she'd be interested."

"And why is that? Are you letting Joe's bullshit fuck with your head?"

"No, she's beautiful, maybe in her mid-twenties."

"She's got that sexy southern debutante thing going on?"

"I don't know, she's—"

"Gideon, you're letting your ex into your head. You're handsome, sweet, intelligent, well off due to a business you worked your ass off to build."

"You don't have to talk me up."

She really didn't. He knew he wasn't unattractive, but Harper was gorgeous.

Something about meeting her troubled him though. He'd stopped outside the window to take one more look. Harper had deflated, her shoulders drooped, and she seemed to pull into herself. The tangible sadness had caused his chest to ache.

It had taken everything in him to walk away. He lived the life of a hermit by choice, but that didn't mean he liked it.

"Gideon," Carol calling his name pulled him from his thoughts.

"Sorry, early to bed, early to rise and all that."

"You're acclimating to the country life well."

"I have been here two years now."

"Come for a visit soon, please?"

"I'll see what I can do."

"You tell me that every time I ask."

"I promise I'll see what I can do. I've got to crash out."

"Fine, I'll call earlier next time so you can't use having to go to bed as an excuse to stop talking to me."

"That's not what I'm doing. I'm harvesting tomorrow."

"Fine. Good night, Gideon."

Ghost said good night and set his phone aside. The deep rumbling of a motorcycle grew louder and then ceased across the yard. He watched as Joker dismounted and slowly walked toward the porch.

"Hey, Ghost."

"Joker, what brings you out here?"

"Got any beer?"

"You know where it is."

Joker didn't say another word just pulled open the screen door and disappeared inside. A few minutes later, Joker came back outside and took a seat in the rocker next to his. The man wasn't much of a talker and to be honest no one knew much about him, except Joker wasn't a man to fuck with and if Joker smiled everyone knew shit was about to go down.

"Something on your mind?"

"Naw, man, shit went nuclear at Brawlers, I bounced out before the cops showed."

"When doesn't things go nuclear there?"

"True. Pelter has a hard-on for all that law and order bullshit. Fucker's ruining everyone's fun."

Joker wasn't a fan of the new Sheriff. The two of them started butting heads even before the man took the job. "I think that's the point of being a Sheriff."

"The old one didn't give a fuck."

"That's because he was corrupt as hell. He nearly took out half the Brawlers Crew."

"Scary and Tank wouldn't let that shit go down. Fucker threatened their husband. You don't do that shit to men like Scary and Tank and expect to get away with it."

"You crashing here tonight?"

"No, gotta get home soon. Got a custom job starting in the morning."

"Well, I have harvesting in the morning. Make yourself at home."

"Thanks, man."

"No problem."

Ghost pushed to his feet and walked around Joker, then he opened the screen door. He turned back to see his friend staring off into the distance. An almost sad look on his face. He started to ask if Joker was okay but knew the answer he'd get. Instead, he went inside to get ready for bed. Tomorrow was a new day. Maybe he needed to make it back to Nightingale's. Maybe Harper would like to have coffee. He shook his head. There were always the maybes. He was damn sick of them. It was time he stopped being so much of a hermit. Not everyone was like his ex. He just wanted someone of his own.

3 Handfasting

Harper watched the happy couple dance around the floor with eyes only for each other. Even though she was ecstatic for her friends, she also felt jealousy. She had always been this contradiction. She dreamed of that happily ever after. Finding her Prince Charming as it were, but in the end, she settled for her own personal hell. Someone to punish her for her so-called sins. Who would inflict the pain she wasn't able to? She shook her head and retreated into the shadows for a walk.

She avoided the people littered along the shadows and headed in the opposite direction of the house. Even though the sun already set, she knew the woods by heart. She'd spent her teens hiding there. Her family hadn't been the demonstrative sort, and they ignored her from the moment she'd said she was a girl. Kyle and his family had taken her in for the nights she was hungry and cold. Kyle had held her as she'd cried when she'd scraped together enough for her first dress. It had been the first and last moment she'd truly felt happiness.

She kept walking as moonlight illuminated her way. She ignored the flashes of lightning and the loud cracks of thunder.

A break in the trees opened onto a large field. Rows upon rows of vegetables and fruit trees. The house in the distance was dark, so she strode forward as the sky opened up. Cool rain quickly drenched her clothes, but she didn't care, as she walked between the rows. Her fingers caressed leaves, some smooth in texture, some fuzzy and velvety. The rain came down so hard that it almost took her breath, but still she walked.

Mud pulled at her feet, and she lifted her one foot then the other to remove her ballet flats. She smiled as soil squished between her toes. Everyone thought she was crazy, so she didn't resist as she held her arms out, tipped her head back and the shower of rain cascaded over her face.

"This storm is about to get worse."

She screamed and spun to find a man cloaked in a slicker. The hood concealed his face.

"Sorry, I'm Gideon, remember me?" He pushed the hood back.

A handsome face with a thick, ginger beard came into view, and she instantly recognized him.

"Oh, O'Brien Shaw."

She remembered him. Sometimes she found herself thinking about the big man with his kind green eyes. It was stupid, but she couldn't stop it. She hadn't had a lot of people be nice to her, and she remembered each one.

"Yes."

"I'm…"

"Don't apologize. I've stood in the rain quite a few times since I planted this field two years ago. But why don't you come inside and dry off? Did you break down?"

She pushed the heavy weight of her wet hair away from her face.

"No, I was at a Handfasting and decided to take a walk."

"Have you had dinner?"

"No, I left before the feast."

"Come on, then, you're not a vegetarian, are you? I was going to throw some steaks on the grill."

"I don't want to impose."

"Not an imposition. You can follow me back to the house, get dried off, have a little dinner, and I'll drive you back to your car once this lets up."

Part of her wanted to say no, but that's not what came out when she opened her mouth. "Okay."

He was being nice. She doubted it would last, but if he'd lived there as long as he had, then he knew about her. In small towns, secrets didn't stay hidden long. If not, she would be selfish and just accept his kindness.

He turned and walked away. He walked slow enough where she easily caught up with him. Gideon didn't walk in front or behind her, if she slowed down, he did too. She sensed he was trying to be non-threatening. She tripped, his arm shot out, and she wrapped her hands around his forearm steadying herself. He didn't try to grab her.

"You're not wearing shoes, be careful. You want me to carry you?"

Panic warred with an almost giddiness of him offering to carry her. Being picked up hadn't ended well for her in the past.

"No, no, I'm fine, thank you."

"Okay, just be careful."

The house came into view, and it was perfect. It was a two-story farmhouse with a huge wraparound porch. A porch swing on the left side wildly swung with the strong wind. Hanging baskets of colorful and fragrant flowers hung from the eaves. She was suddenly excited to see inside. It was like her dream house. She quickened her steps and left Gideon behind, she practically jogged up the steps. She paused with her hand on the screen door, tensing as she realized what she'd done.

Rich, laughter came from behind her. "Go on in. The door's unlocked. The light switch is on the right side just as you go in."

She opened the door and stepped inside, the house smelled like spicy incense and men's cologne. It was a comforting scent. And she drew it in through her nose as she flipped the switch. She took several steps forward as she turned to look into the first room she came to.

It was perfect. The subtle natural tones were punctuated by a colorful quilt on the back of the huge couch. Beautiful splashes of vibrant shades on canvas littered the walls.

"Oh, I'm dripping all over your floors and getting mud everywhere."

"You're fine, it'll dry, Harper. The kitchen is straight back. I have some towels in the laundry room."

She glanced over her shoulder to see him motioning her forward.

She carefully made her way toward the kitchen. She stepped into the darkened room, and the lights turned on. The kitchen was a mix of traditional farmhouse and modern steel. She knew she was probably embarrassing herself with the awe she was showing. There was no way she could hide it. She'd never been that close to a dream before.

Gideon walked passed her, and she noticed he'd removed his jacket. Flannel stretched across his wide shoulders and back. His hair was wet and combed back, the sides shaved while the top was wavy and long. She shivered as fear at his size caused her to step back.

"You're cold, I know it's spring, but I can start a fire or turn on the heat."

"No, I don't want to be a bother."

"Never a bother. I think I have some sweats and a t-shirt, they'll be really big on you, but the pants have a drawstring. Do you want to take a shower to warm up? I can wait on dinner until you're done."

She noticed he was looking everywhere but at her. She looked down to find her white, summer dress nearly transparent. She crossed her arms over her chest. She was deficient in the breast department so she never really wore a bra.

"I'll be fine after I dry off and get into some dry clothes."

"Let me get you the towel and clothes, then I'll show you to the bathroom."

He disappeared and returned minutes later with a pile of clothes.

"You lucked out, the dryer just stopped, and the towels are all warm. Follow me."

He led her to a back staircase off the kitchen. The narrow passage made her claustrophobic, but thankfully, they quickly entered a bedroom. A huge bed stood in the center of the room. Windows ran the full length of one wall.

She watched him as he laid the pile on the end of the bed.

"Bathroom is through there. Take your time. If you want to shower, help yourself. I'll start dinner, just come down when you're ready."

He seemed like he wanted to say something else, but stopped himself. Gideon walked back toward the stairs.

"Harper, you don't know me, and I get your nervous, but you're safe here. I won't make promises because you probably won't believe me."

She just nodded, and she listened to his heavy steps. She relaxed as she realized he'd done it on purpose to prove he'd left. She grabbed the towel and rushed to the bathroom. Her wet clothes were becoming uncomfortable.

She quickly removed her soaked dress and panties as she looked at the huge glass-enclosed shower stall. The damn thing was bigger than her whole bathroom at her apartment. He did say she could take a shower.

Giggling, she reached inside and turned the taps and water cascaded from several shower heads. She might never have another chance to spend time in a place like that, and she wanted to take advantage. She avoided looking at the mirror and stepped inside. She moaned at the pressure. Using Gideon's shampoo and body wash was weird, but she pushed it away.

An odd thought hit her, she liked his scent on her. Her breathing increased, and her heart kicked against her ribs. Pleasure followed the caress of her palms, and her nipples tightened. She looked down to find them hard, and her eyes burned as she stared at her semi-erection. She avoided touching herself. It had been years since she masturbated and it wouldn't be in some stranger's shower.

She enjoyed the last of her shower and stepped out, the thick, soft towel was heaven on her skin. She dried off, finger combed her hair and went to get dressed so she could head downstairs.

With her clothes rolled in the towel, she went to find Gideon. The back door was open, and she could see him standing on the porch as he stared off into the distance.

"Gideon?"

"Enjoy your shower?" He smiled as he asked.

"It was amazing. I think your shower is bigger than my whole bathroom." She felt her face flush as she said it.

"First thing I did was renovate the bathroom. I also made my bedroom a sanctuary. The only other way out is through a door at the back of the closet. I'm the only one here, but I like my privacy."

"Your house is beautiful."

"Thank you."

"You said you lived here two years."

"Yeah, my cousin, Gregory, suggested I move here when I needed a change."

"Bull's Gregory?"

"Bull's Gregory. That still gets me every time."

"He's a possessive man when it comes to his husband."

"Yes, he is, and Gregory doesn't mind at all. Can't deny the love between them though."

She'd always been jealous of the Crew's husbands. The love was tangible. It was like a physical presence whenever she was around them or when she heard them speak of each other.

"No. You have a nickname, but I can't remember."

"Ghost."

"Ghost?"

"They said I'm as elusive as a Ghost. One minute I'm there and the next I'm gone. I don't know if that means I'm forgettable or not."

"You're definitely not forgettable. I mean…"

"Thank you. Did you want a beer or I have tea, iced and hot, some sodas?"

"Iced tea would be great."

"It's looking pretty bad out there," Gideon said as he stepped inside. "Do you have to call someone?"

"Oh, I forgot my purse in my car. I better call Joker, or he'll worry."

"You know Joker?"

"Yes, I don't know why, but he likes to know where I am. If I don't check in, he gets a bit…"

"Homicidal."

"You know Joker."

"Here," Gideon reached into his back pocket and pulled out his phone. He held it out to her.

"Are you sure?"

"Actually, his number is the last one I called. How do you like your steak?"

"However you make…"

"How do you like your steak?"

"Medium rare."

"Good, make your call."

She didn't leave the room. It wasn't like the call would be private. She stroked her fingers over the screen and tapped the phone icon, then connected the call. She listened to it ring.

"Ghost, what the fuck do you want?"

"Your phone etiquette amazes me."

"What the fuck are you doing calling from Ghost's phone?"

"I took a walk…"

"In the rain. Do you need me to come get you?"

"No, Gideon said he'd drive me back to my car when the storm lets up."

"Did someone say something to you to make you walk?"

"Joker, I don't have bail money for you."

She smiled as she heard Gideon's snort and looked up to find him watching her with a small grin. She took the tall glass he handed her and mouthed thank you.

"I don't always need bail money."

"Whatever you say, I just wanted to check in. Last time I didn't, I don't think the sale's lady at the store has recovered. She looks for you every time I go in."

"I asked her nicely where the fuck you were."

"We're not arguing."

"I'm not arguing. I'm stating a fact."

"Joker, leave her alone so I can make her dinner."

"Make sure he's gentlemanly, I don't want to have to kill a friend."

Harper rolled her eyes and said goodbye. She disconnected the call and handed Gideon his phone back.

"Did you need to call anyone else?"

"No, thank you. You'll take me back to my car soon."

"Come sit on the porch while I cook."

She nodded and followed him, the screened porch kept out most of the rain except for mist brought in by the wind. She curled up on one side of a second swing.

"Have you always been a farmer?"

"Not at all. The most I had was a small garden and helped out at a community garden."

"Then why start a farm?"

"I always found gardening to be relaxing. Why not buy my own and do it on a larger scale?"

"There had to be a reason."

"I was with someone for a long time. They weren't faithful, and I forgave them until they left. I owned a large event planning company. I enjoyed it at first, but after a while, people demanded more and more. After my breakup, I really didn't have a reason to stay. I left the company in the capable hands of my partner and moved here."

"I'm sorry about your breakup."

"It would've happened sooner or later, I should've ended it after the first affair, but I was young and in love."

"I've never been in love."

"You're a beautiful woman, you'll find someone when the time is right."

"I don't know. I've lived in this town my whole life. Secrets don't stay secret."

"Haven't you ever thought of leaving?"

"I did…went away to college. It didn't last, you know the old saying, the Devil you know is better than the Devil you don't."

She sipped her tea as Gideon turned away and turned the steaks, the scent caused her stomach to growl.

"Hungry, that's good. I picked some vegetables before the storm hit. So, there's salad, grilled vegetables and steak."

"I don't eat that much in a week. I live on Ben's coffee."

"He does make some damn good coffee."

"Yes, he does, I swear I only work to pay my caffeine habit. Do you need help? I feel lazy just sitting here."

"No, you sit and relax, I got dinner covered. Maybe next time you can cook."

"Next time?"

"You're welcome out here anytime. Maybe you can see the fields during the day, and I can show you the greenhouse. You like flowers?"

"I love flowers."

"Then maybe you can come out one day, and I'll show you around."

"I sit with Nettie, Crave's mom, during the week before I go to work. I usually have the weekends off unless Clora needs me to work Saturday for her."

"Unless The Executioners are playing a gig, I'm usually free Saturday, and I'm always off on Sunday. The invitation is open anytime."

"Okay, that's very nice of you."

"What are new friends for?"

She spent the evening talking and relaxed, and enjoyed an easy meal with Gideon. When the storm finally let up, she didn't want to leave. It was the first time in her life she felt safe. Comfortable in her own skin without worrying about the next hit. She wasn't stupid or broken, at least she tried to pretend she wasn't those things. And something else odd happened, she wanted her first kiss and was almost devastated when Gideon simply said goodnight. She'd love a new friend, and that would have to be enough.

4 Harper's Lips Were Too Much Temptation

Ghost's fingers combed through the hair on his chest, then on his stomach as he stared up at the ceiling. The sun was just cresting the horizon and illuminated his room. He hadn't slept at all last night thinking of Harper's full, pink lips and her shy smiles. When he'd dropped her off, all he'd wanted to do was kiss her. Her nervousness stopped him.

He lifted his arm to cover his eyes with his forearm. She had smiled and laughed, except for that one moment when she froze on his porch. The light had disappeared, but once it came back, she was more beautiful than before. He wanted to hold and touched her. Instead of doing what he'd wanted, he tried to talk to her—learn about Harper. She'd avoided the personal questions preferring to talk about books, movies or him.

Before he'd closed her door when he'd dropped her off, he opened his mouth to ask her on a date. What had he done instead? Told her goodnight and closed her door. He had watched her until the taillights of her shitty little compact car disappeared. The thing had barely started, and he'd wanted to follow her home just to make sure she got there.

His alarm went off interrupting his thoughts, and he reached out slapping the off button. It was Sunday, but he loved his routine and was always up by six. Which normally meant if he and the band had gigs, he went without sleep, but it was his day off so he could be lazy. Although, a smile tugged at the corners of his mouth as he rolled from bed and went to take a shower.

Two years of being cautious. Rethinking every decision he'd ever made, especially when it came to his decisions on his dismal love life. Maybe it was time to take a chance. Carol, Twitch, Gregory, Sin and Saint were driving him crazy to start dating. He was only interested in one person, and he wanted to spend time with her. But first, he needed information. Some advice from the person who seemed to know her best—Joker.

#

"Fuck you," Joker barked never looking up from the cluttered top of his desk.

The man despised office work, but he refused to hire someone to do it. No one was in a particular hurry to jump at the job.

"Come on, man, help me out, all I need is a phone number. I'm not asking for an address." He plopped down in the chair in front of Joker's desk. He rested his bearded cheek in his palm and braced his elbow on the arm.

"You're not getting your dick anywhere near Harper. Not fucking happening."

He was starting to get a bit insulted. He had always assumed he was a nice guy.

"I wasn't planning to—"

"She said she was naked at your place."

"She was soaked from the rain. She took a shower to warm up. We were not naked in the same space."

He couldn't believe he had to explain that to one of his best friends, or thought was his best friend.

"So, you don't find Harper beautiful?"

Joker logic just made him dizzy. One minute he wasn't supposed to fuck Harper and the next he was in trouble because he possibly didn't find her attractive.

"She's gorgeous. Sweet. Quiet. Skittish. I just wanted to ask her out to the farm for lunch. I don't plan to get her in my bed anytime soon or at all. It would just be nice to spend time with her."

"You know about her, right?"

"What about her? She didn't talk much about herself last night." That was one of the reasons he wanted to take her out. Maybe if he could just have the opportunity to talk to her on the phone, she could become more comfortable with him.

"She has shit taste in men."

He didn't remember much about the stories he'd heard about Harper. She acted as a caretaker for Nettie, Crave's mom. She babysat the Crew's kids. They loved spending time with their Aunt Harper. Again, the stories weren't prevalent, everyone was entitled to their privacy. One thing he'd learned was there were rumors that a local bigot loved to take his anger out on her. He had a feeling it was more than that, but again no one shared.

"It's lunch, not a marriage proposal."

"You're going to lose teeth."

Joker didn't joke, it was why the man got the nickname he did.

"Jackson." He waited for the man to turn away from his paperwork. "I like her. What's wrong with that? It's lunch. New friends getting to know each other. What's the harm in giving me her number?"

"No one is—"

"Joker?"

He turned his head to find Harper standing in the doorway of Joker's office. Rage and Gunner, Psycho's twins, perched on her hips. They're hands tangled in her long blonde hair. He stood and gave her a smile as he approached.

"Hi, Harper, want me to take one of them," he asked.

"Yes, Rage is trying to snatch me bald."

"Can't have that. Come on, Rage, let's give Aunt Harper's scalp a break." He held out his hands and waited for the toddler to make up his mind. It was well-known among the Crews Rage didn't like a lot of people. Luckily, he was one of the ones Rage tolerated.

The chunky boy lunged forward. Bright green eyes stared up at him, and he smiled as he held Rage against his chest. Rage was a terrible nickname for a kid, but the boy had a temper and as vocal about who and what he didn't like. They were going to have to start calling Rage by his real name before the boy went off to school. He didn't know what was wrong with the name Thomas, it was perfectly fine and normal name.

"Thank you."

"You're welcome. I'm glad to see you. I was trying to get Joker to give me your number."

"Why," she asked, bouncing Gunner on her hip as the boy tried to get to his twin.

Rage and Gunner couldn't deal with being away from each other. Getting out of each other's sight was an instant meltdown in the making.

"I was hoping I could take you to lunch or dinner."

Her pretty eyes widened. "Why?"

He tightened his arms around Rage to keep from reaching for Harper. Her shock at him wanting to spend time with her saddened him.

"Because I like you."

"O…oh, like friends?"

"I was kind of looking at it like asking you on a date, but friends would be great too. No pressure, Harper. Lunch or dinner, maybe a picnic at the farm. I'll show you around the greenhouse."

He didn't like when she looked away and down at her bare toes. The nails were painted a pale pink to match her long, loose dress that fell to her ankles. He curled his fingers into his palms to keep himself from stroking her cheek and lifting her gaze to his.

"You want to take me on a…date?"

She didn't look at him as she asked the question. He knew he had to be patient with Harper. What he did know of her past wasn't pretty. He sensed no one outside of the Crew treated her with kindness—touched her gently. Loved on her. He wouldn't lie especially to himself, he wanted her. He just didn't know if she could let down her guard enough to let him in.

"Yes, but if you don't want to, all you have to do is say no."

"I don't…don't know."

He forced his smile to stay in place. "Why don't you just come out for a picnic? Just friends."

"O…okay."

"You can bring the twins."

"I was just coming to ask Joker to take me to drop them off. My car wouldn't start."

"We can get their car seats in the backseat of my truck."

"Harper, I'll go over to your place and tow it in." Joker was up from his desk before he finished talking.

The man would make any excuse to avoid office work.

"I can't—"

"I'll tow it in."

Harper's pale cheeks turned pink with embarrassment. He knew she was going to protest because she couldn't afford to get her car fixed.

"Did you want me to walk over with you to get their car seats? That way you don't have to carry them both back."

"Thank you."

They said their goodbyes to Joker as they exited the shop and made their way down the block. Harper kept a good distance between them. He tried to pretend it didn't hurt. He knew patience was key. He'd just met her, but he knew she was worth whatever he had to do to earn her trust. First step, spending some alone time with Harper, everything else would work itself out.

5 Was This What a Date Was?

Harper twisted her blonde hair into a loose bun as she stood in Ghost's kitchen. She curled her toes into the thick area rug. The house still smelled of incense and cologne, with hints of body wash coming from Ghost. She tucked a few stray curls behind her ears and then laced her fingers together.

Ghost wanted to date her, or at least that's what he said. She still didn't understand. Her brain kept coming up with every ulterior motive, but if he just wanted to fuck her, why was he being so nice. No one else had taken the time to do more than turn her away and bend her over. They didn't look at her. Kiss her. They didn't caress her like she mattered.

She closed her eyes as she imagined what being loved would be like. She didn't imagine sex. Kisses, hugs, and cuddling—she had always found herself jealous of the couples she saw who just—touched as if that was all they needed.

"Harper?"

She opened her eyes and saw Ghost watching her with concern.

"I'm sorry."

"Harper, you're fine. Are you okay?"

"Tired, the twins are active."

Ghost's laughter was deep and attractive, she realized she loved the sound of it.

"They definitely are. They've been out here a few times. Would you like to lay down for a nap? I can make dinner when you get up."

"I...I couldn't do that, it would be—"

"Not rude, if you're tired, I don't mind. Come on," Ghost said and held out his hand.

She nervously nibbled at her lip.

"I promise you're just going to take a nap."

"I'm being stupid."

Ghost's calloused hands took hers. She dropped her gaze to see her slender hands engulfed in his. His skin was warm and rough, yet gentle.

"You're not stupid. I'll get you all tucked in, and then I'll go pick you some flowers. Have a favorite color?"

"I've always liked purple."

She let him lead her toward the stairs to his room. He didn't tug roughly. It was almost like last night when he'd walked beside her. She liked he didn't stand behind her or push her forward. Her stomach jumped and twisted with nerves, but not fear. It was an odd thing to not be afraid; she was always scared.

They stepped into Ghost's bedroom. The huge bed was unmade which she found weird. A smile pulled at the corner of her mouth. She almost held onto his hand when he pulled away but didn't want to embarrass herself.

"Sorry, it's a mess, I didn't take the time to make the bed. I was trying to get to Joker before he disappeared."

She watched as he bent over the bed and straightened the sheets. His t-shirt stretched across his broad back. He fluffed the pillows and stood.

"He does have a tendency to hide out when he wants to avoid people."

"Lay down."

"I don't sleep."

"Then you definitely need to lie down, even if you don't sleep, you can relax."

"I don't know how."

"This is all it takes," Ghost said and laid down on the right side, then patted the spot beside him.

"I thought—"

"Nothing is going to happen."

"Do you know—"

"You're a beautiful woman, that's all I need to know unless you want to share. I didn't sleep last night."

She walked to the opposite side of the bed, and she hesitated for a few minutes before she took the spot beside him. A sigh slipped passed her lips at the feel of the firm, comfortable mattress. It was so different from the lumpy futon she's slept on for the past few years since she was able to afford her own place. Most of her furniture was hand-me-downs or thrift store finds. The pillows were fluffy and not flattened down, she could get used to this bed.

"I scraped together spare change until I could afford my first dress."

"What did it look like?"

"It was peach and so soft, it was from a thrift store, but I was so happy."

"I'm sure you looked gorgeous. I don't think I've ever seen you in pants."

"I love dresses."

Was there something wrong with her dresses? She always felt pretty in them. Being skinny, she didn't have a lot of curves; the dresses made her feel feminine.

"I wasn't criticizing you for your dresses. My whole wardrobe consists of jeans and t-shirts, I don't think I've worn a suit since I moved here."

"I bet you look handsome in a suit." Her face heated yet she tried to ignore her embarrassment.

She turned her head on the pillow and watched as Ghost rolled to his side. She couldn't get over how handsome he was, but the part she was hung up on was how nice he was being to her. Not once did she have the urge to flinch or protect herself. Even with the Crews, who she had come to consider family, she couldn't let her guard down. Always waiting to wear out her welcome.

"I always felt like I was playing dress up. Appearances were everything. It was tiring."

She frowned at the sadness in his voice. He always seemed to be smiling. It was disconcerting to see the man unhappy; she didn't like it. She decided to change the subject.

"What was it like living in New York City?"

She occasionally went to Atlanta to shop with Twitch or Elijah. Sometimes she thought about packing up and moving back, somewhere she could be invisible or start over.

"Noisy."

"Tell me the good things."

"Well…" Ghost shifted closer. "I grew up there. Everything was normal. There were the shows. Galleries.

Parties, but there were also the mundane things that happen everywhere no matter big city or small town. Since I moved here, I found I liked the quiet and laid-back pace."

"Do you ever get lonely out here," she asked as she rolled to face him, hugging the pillow to her chest.

She didn't feel like she needed a shield against Ghost, but years of guarding herself against violence and pain putting something between them was an involuntary response.

"Everyone gets lonely."

"If you don't want—"

"It isn't that I don't want to answer, I'm just trying to come up with a response that doesn't make me sound pathetic."

"You couldn't sound pathetic."

"Gregory invited me here to meet Bull, I always said I had too much to do. The truth was, I was miserable and hiding."

"Did you love your partner?"

Calloused roughened fingertips danced along the back of her hand. She clenched her fingers around the pillow to disguise the shaking. She hid her face as his fingers eased between hers.

"I was an eighteen-year-old kid, I thought I loved him—"

"But?"

She quietly chuckled when he sighed and rolled to his back, yet he never let go of her hand. He seemed to hold on a little tighter while his thumb stroked over her skin. She knew it was silly, but she couldn't help the butterflies that circled in her stomach. She stayed on her side and studied his profile. His beard was long and thick, perfectly groomed. His chest powerful and his belly rounded and yet firm. She wondered what it would be like to curl up against his side. She'd never cuddled before, she wondered—

"I loved him in the beginning, then he cheated the first time. I was in my early twenties. I forgave him, but it was never the same. After a while, it turns into routine."

"I'm sorry."

"No need to be sorry. Why don't you talk about yourself more?"

"I'm not all that interesting."

"You might not think so. Would you mind if I asked you some questions? You can always refuse to answer."

"O…okay."

"You're a nurse, why don't you work at the local clinic?"

"I didn't finish. I had an—"

"You had a what?"

"I was going to say accident. I had to drop out and just never went back." She glanced at the leather of her cuffs. Thick and dark brown, just wide enough to hide everything but the edges of her scars. "It wasn't my calling. I love sitting with Nettie though. Her lucid moments are longer now."

"Why wasn't it your calling," he asked.

"I don't know. I loved the caretaker aspect, but I wasn't crazy about the blood."

"Understandable."

"What do you want from me?"

She flinched, rolled to her back and froze before the question had completely passed her lips. Her survival instinct kicked in and she prepared for the hit she was sure was coming. Her respiration increased as fear stole through her. It was always the first mistake, the justification for the first slap or punch. No, not justification, she didn't deserve—

"Hey, look at me please," Ghost implored.

He was so close his breath caressed her cheek, and his palm cupped her opposite one, gently urged her to turn toward him. She kept her eyes tightly closed. Trusting the tenderness of his tone warred with her inherent urge to survive.

"Okay, you don't have to look at me, just listen."

Ghost's beard and mustache tickled her cheek as his firm lips brushed the sensitive skin below her ear.

"At this moment, I don't want anything from you, just this. Conversation, your presence, your smile and rare laughs. One day I'll want a date, in the outside world, holding your hand and not see this…" His rough fingertip stroked the grooves she knew were between her brows. "On your face. I like you. I think you're beautiful. And one day I hope you'll believe me. That's it, no ulterior motives. I only want to spend time with you."

The warm tickle of tears from under her lashes and slipping down her cheeks preceded a sob she barely concealed.

"Shh, Harper," Ghost whispered.

Her cries increased as he kissed away the salty drops of her tears at the corner of her right eye.

"It's okay, come here."

Ghost's voice was gentle, filled with a tenderness she'd never heard directed at her before. He rolled her toward him with a soft pressure on her hip and her body laid fully against his. Her flat stomach conformed to the firm curve of his, and his powerful rounded pecs pressed to her small breasts. One of his thighs were as thick as both of hers. She trembled uncontrollably at the overwhelming sensation of being held for the first time in years—if ever.

She had never felt as delicate as she did as his large hand splayed across her lower back.

"You're probably exhausted, how about we just take a nap and when we wake up, I'll make us some food."

She couldn't answer around the knot in her throat and did something she had always wanted to do, she cuddled. She shifted into closer contact with Ghost. Absorbed his warmth, the smoky scent of his skin and nuzzled his beard with her forehead. A small smile pulled at her mouth as his beard tickled her nose and all she could do was move closer. She didn't want to think about anything other than that moment. A memory she could hold onto when Ghost grew tired of her, and she needed something to remind her that, at one time, she was safe.

6 Be Patient, Ghost, This is Harper's Show

The sweet fragrance of flowers and rich soil surrounded him as he sat at his workbench in his greenhouse and created the perfect bouquet for Harper. Keeping his hands busy kept him from reaching for the phone to call her. They exchanged texts throughout the day, he called in the evenings to check how her day was, but the last time he'd spoken to her was two days ago.

He knew he needed to be patient. His heart broke when she'd asked what he wanted from her. When she'd started to cry, all he could do was hold her. He wanted her story. Her trust. It needed to be Harper's show, her pace, however slow that might be.

He wasn't some Alpha male like most of his friends. He was quiet and unassuming. He didn't have the bad boy allure. He had lived with his one and only for eighteen years. It hadn't all been bad times, but most of it had. Their time together had been them leading separate lives. He had his business and friends, Joe had his Accounting Firm and innumerable lovers. They'd turned into roommates. No love existed between them, sometimes not even like.

He laid out the colorful arrangement and wrapped it in brown paper, then tied it with twine. It was a mix of pinks, purples, and bright greens. It was made with every plant he'd noticed she touched when he showed her around his greenhouse Sunday. Tulips, Lavender, Pink Roses, Lilac and several more. It was a large bouquet, but he wanted to make her something over the top.

He'd also ordered her the perfect orchid from a friend in New York.

"That's gorgeous," Twitched squealed behind him.

He turned to find Twitch bouncing. The young man was always so happy and positive. He'd learned that hadn't always been the case.

"Is that for Harper," Twitched asked with a wide smile.

He gently caressed the soft petals. "Yes, it is. Do you think she'll like it?"

"She'll love it. And why did I have to hear from Joker you've been dating Harper?"

"We're not dating, as much as I wish, she hasn't said yes to anything more than a dinner last Sunday."

"That's huge though, Harper's very introverted. Other than spending time with Nettie or when we drag her out to hang out with us, she spends the rest of her time working."

"Yeah, I kinda got that feeling." He set the bouquet aside and stood, turning toward Twitch.

"You're going to have to be patient."

"This I know."

44

He crossed his arms over his chest and leaned back on the edge of his worktable.

"Why didn't anyone ever try—"

"We all tried. We invited her to Crew events. When she sits with Nettie, we try to get her to stay longer just to talk. Joker has threatened the life of every person who even looked at her sideways."

"Why—"

"Harper is only a few years older than me, and I remembered her growing up. Current life and past, she's always been small and delicate, they said she was premature like me. She was always sweet and quiet, and they gave her hell in school. That didn't change after she graduated. Harper earned a scholarship for college. She was only gone a year before she was back."

"Why did she come back?"

"Probably the usual story, it wasn't different outside the limits of Powers, same shit different bullies."

"She said the other night, the Devil you know—"

"Is better than the one you don't. Harper is this amazing woman who doesn't see it."

"So, me telling her—"

"You have to show her, Ghost, by being you. Sweet and charming, considerate. I'm pretty positive men haven't ever been like that with her even when all they wanted to do was fuck her."

"I don't want to fuck her."

Twitch arched a perfectly groomed brow.

"Don't be an asshole, you've been with Crave way too long. Yes, I find her extremely sexually attractive, but that isn't all I see."

"You're too easy, of course you don't see her as some sex toy for your Alpha male cock strong bullshit."

"Alpha, I'm not."

"I'm pretty sure you have it in you, but that's neither here nor there at the moment. I have a favor to ask."

"Oh shit, what?"

"You're so fucking suspicious."

Twitch placed his hands on his slim hips and cocked one to the side. The little impish grin made him nervous and slightly terrified.

"Justifiably so."

"Ha ha, I checked with King, you don't have another gig for a few weeks. Psycho and Ben's anniversary is coming up, Stacey and Bernie deserve a break, with Brawlers and all we don't have—"

"I'll watch the twins and Sawyer."

Psycho, Ben, Bernie, and Stacey's youngest, Sawyer, was only a few months old. The co-parenting relationship between the two couples fascinated him in the fact they made it seem so effortless.

He'd watched the Crew's kids plenty over the last two years. He was like the go-to babysitter, and he loved it when the kids would run around and play in the fields.

"You're the fucking best. We've already rented the cabins and arranged for romantic dinners, it's perfectly planned. Stacey has pumped and frozen enough milk for a few days."

"I'm sure we'll be fine. When do I get them?"

"Next weekend, we'll drop them off Friday night and pick up Sunday."

"I'll need all their gear."

"We'll make sure you have everything, and if an emergency comes up, Elijah or me will bring whatever you need. You going to drop that off or did you want me to deliver your girl some flowers?"

"Would you? I'm trying to be patient, and I don't want to—"

"Crowd her when she isn't ready?"

"Yeah, that."

"Write her a little note to go along with those flowers."

He grinned and turned to his bench. He wished he had something prettier than a yellow notepad. He grabbed a pen in his left hand and quickly jotted down a note. Carefully he folded it and slipped it between the brown paper and flowers, then he held out the bouquet.

"I'll drop them off on my way to see Nettie."

"Thanks, Twitch."

"I love playing matchmaker."

He chuckled as Twitch bounced yet held the flowers carefully.

"Don't get those hopes up too high. She might not even see me the way I want her to."

"Impossible, you've got that sexy, cuddly Prince Charming thing going for you."

"Thanks, I think."

"Shut up, man, you got this. Now, let me make this important delivery."

Twitch hugged him and held on for a few minutes, he gently stroked the younger man's back. The man loved affection. Crave was pretty possessive of his husband, but when Crave wasn't around, Twitch found comfort in his friends.

He walked Twitch to his car, said goodbye and he watched Twitch until the small vehicle disappeared at the end of the driveway. He wondered what Harper would think of his gift. Maybe the arrangement was too big, but it had all the flowers she seemed to like.

He sighed as he turned to head back to his greenhouse. He wouldn't agonize over it. Harper deserved to be treated like she mattered. He didn't want to hope for too much. Yes, she'd allowed him to hold her as she slept. Let him hold her hand as they walked through his fields and greenhouse.

Harper was innocent and skittish, even with the life she'd led, she still blushed at something as innocent as him holding her hand. She needed romance and tenderness, and that was just what he was going to give her. Because the woman he liked deserved it all.

7 She had Never Gotten Flowers Before

Ghost had picked her flowers, arranged the most beautiful bouquet she had ever seen, and she didn't know how to process. She had wanted to call him so many times since Sunday. She's woken to find her face tucked against his neck and his arms tight around her. She buried her face in the flowers and inhaled.

"He wrote you a note."

She glanced up to find Twitch smiling at her, and his eyes twinkled. Her fingers shook as she found the yellow paper. She kept the flowers on her lap as she unfolded the note.

Miss the sound of your voice, please call when you're ready. Hope you like the flowers. G.

"He likes you."

"But why?"

She still didn't understand. She wasn't special or all that pretty, her body was a roadmap of scar tissue, and more often than not, bruises. She couldn't remember the last time she'd looked at her naked body for more than a glance.

"Don't start your bullshit, Harper. Ghost is the premier catch around here. He doesn't think so, but he's been coming into Brawlers for years and never once—"

"He's gay?"

"I don't think gender really matters to him. As far as I know, he's Bi."

"Maybe he won't find me attractive if—"

"Stop it!"

She jerked her gaze up to find Twitch pulling at his long, dark hair. She bent forward to place her flowers on the coffee table.

"What?"

"You're devising all these what-if scenarios in your head. He's a nice guy. Picked flowers and arranged them. Sent them through me because he doesn't want to crowd you if you're not ready."

She made sure the sidewalk outside was deserted. The only way she was going to get any advice she needed was by opening up, but that wasn't exactly her style.

"We cuddled," she blurted out.

"Was he a gentleman?"

"Yes."

"Come on, Harper, details, woman, details," Twitch demanded.

She laughed softly as Twitch started bouncing. The man was way too excitable. She loved Twitch, but sometimes the man was exhausting.

"There's nothing to give details about. He let me take a nap, and I cuddled up to him. Just held me."

"Did you like it?"

"I don't...don't know."

"What don't you know about?"

Just as she was about to answer she didn't know again, the chime over the door drew her attention. A tall, lanky man with impeccable hair and a rumpled suit walked in. She smiled at her best friend, Kyle, the man was a mess.

"What are you doing here?"

"Do I need an excuse to see my best friend in the whole world," Kyle asked.

"Yes, especially when it's the middle of the day, and you're normally chained to your desk."

Kyle flopped down beside her and fell to the side to lay his head on her lap. She rolled her eyes, and he batted his lashes.

"We've been friends since first grade, and I know those fluttering lashes well."

"I'm hearing these rumors."

"It's a small town, which rumors would you be speaking about?"

"A certain beautiful blonde has been spending some time with a certain ginger farmer who plays in a band."

"And how would you...Joker."

"Didn't take you long to answer your own question."

"Joker's a bigger gossip than anyone I've ever met." Twitch grabbed his huge to-go cup with both hands.

Twitch plus caffeine or sugar was never a good idea, but she'd assumed Twitch would've already headed home by now. Twitch was a menace on coffee and Ben knew that.

"So, why the hell wasn't I told?"

"There's nothing to tell—"

"That's only because she keeps playing the what-if game and not giving Ghost a chance."

"Ghost?"

"His real name is Gideon."

"Sounds like a Knight in Shining Armor or a Prince Charming."

She rolled her eyes again at Kyle and leaned back into the cushion. She should've never told Kyle about the whole Prince Charming thing, she was eleven at the time. It figured Kyle would never forget it.

"He even cut her flowers." Twitch nodded toward the flowers in question.

"Aw, that's so sweet." Kyle grinned.

"Shut up."

"So when's the first date?"

Twitched answered before she had a chance, "She hasn't accepted, even though he's made her dinner at least twice, cuddled once."

Kyle surged to a sitting position and spun around to stare at her. She fidgeted as he watched her.

"You've cuddled with someone of the male persuasion...actually touching. Tell me there were no clothes involved."

"Yes," she squeaked, "There were clothes."

"I've heard the ginger farmer is pretty hot," Kyle waggled his brows.

"What would you know about—"

"I am secure enough in my sexuality to admit when a man is hot or not, my wife, and you, my friend, have had me surrounded by ladies my entire life."

"You have guy friends."

"What did I do on my last Saturday night off?"

She snorted. "Mud mask, mani and pedi, and your first Brazilian."

"The last I will not be repeating, no matter how much my gorgeous wife enjoyed the smooth landscape that is my nether region. Without the cushion of my mainly bush, wearing my boxer briefs was a rather odd experience."

"Kyle, what have we talked about?"

"Um, I don't remember."

"TMI, Kyle, I have no need to know about your manly bush or lack thereof."

"We're best friends, I tell you everything!"

"I'd appreciate it if you told me less."

"You're no fun."

She caught Kyle winking at a giggling Twitch.

She loved Kyle to death, even had a crush on him when they were kids, and she'd been terrified to tell him about her—that she was a girl. He hadn't even acted surprised just asked what she wanted to be called. She liked her name. They'd named her after her grandmother, the woman had loved her even after she'd confessed who she really was. Her grandmother died her senior year of high school, and Harper decided her given name was perfect as is.

"I need to be invited next time, Crave hasn't done my toes in forever." Twitched pouted. "He sucks at the whole mani thing, but at least he used to try. We've reached old married couple status."

"I'm sure it's not that bad. That man touches you every time he's near you."

Again, jealousy made her focus everywhere but on Twitch or Kyle. She had always been the outsider. Envy was a petty emotion.

She'd never had anyone feel anything for her but condemnation—disgust. A year ago, she decided she didn't want to be Bill's secret—his punching bag—any longer. But he wouldn't leave her alone, and she didn't have anywhere to run. Joker would go to jail if he ever learned the truth. She knew most of them assumed and they were probably right, although as far as anyone knew she was merely Bill's favorite target.

"Y'all have to come out to Brawlers the next time The Executioners play. I swear you haven't seen anything as mesmerizing as Ghost playing his guitar or keyboard."

She'd noticed a piano in his living room, but hadn't asked. Music had been one of her favorite classes in school. She'd learned to play. Not great, but it let her spend time alone in the music room. The most peace she'd experienced was when she played. She wondered if Ghost would let her play sometime.

"Don't say no, Harper. We'll get everyone together, including Peaches, Lily, and Bernie and Stacey, even Lou."

"I'll think about it."

"Kyle, you come and drag her with you."

"I'll see what I can do."

"Okay, I gotta get home, I have to get dinner started, or the guys will revolt and claim they're starving to death."

The Brawlers Crew were notorious for being useless at feeding themselves. She let Twitch kiss her cheek and watched as Kyle offered his own. Her best friend was amazing. Twitch left with a wave over his shoulder.

"So, why haven't you accepted? And no bullshit answer."

She sighed as she reclined and turned to study Kyle.

"He's—"

"From what I've heard around town, the man is nice. Genuine. Maybe a bit reclusive. You don't date, Harper. I know your secret."

"I don't have secrets."

"Harper."

All Kyle needed to do was say her name in that disapproving tone when he knew she lied about something.

"You don't deserve it. I can bitch all I want, me and Marla love you. Just because we aren't blood, you're the sister I had always wanted. Take a chance, honey. A man makes you dinner. Cuts flowers and takes the time to do that…" Kyle pointed at the bundle of flowers. "He's gotta have more in mind than just getting under your dress."

She was about to come up with another excuse, but grabbed Kyle's hand when Bill walked by the window. His dark eyes were filled with rage. He strode slowly by never taking his gaze away from her. Her eyes burned as tears streamed down her cheeks and her heartbeat kicked up steadily into a painful rhythm. A band circled her chest and her vision narrowed into a tunnel as she fought to breathe.

Kyle's voice warbled as she heard him calling her name.

"Breathe, in and out, easy," Kyle cooed. "Tell me something good."

"I don't—"

"Tell me something good."

"Gideon."

"I thought it was Ghost."

"I like Gideon better."

"Okay, what about Gideon?"

"Everything."

"Then what's the damn problem, Harper?"

"I'm scared."

"Of course you are, a nice guy is interested in you, and you're unable to process it. Take a chance on something good for a change, for me, please?"

"What if I'm wrong?"

55

"Honey, our friends are friends with him, do you actually think Twitch would be so excited about a man interested in you if he was an asshole?"

"Gideon is Gregory's cousin."

"Bull would kill someone who was a bastard who got near his husband, family or not."

That was definitely true.

"Gideon wants to take me on a date."

"A date, a real date, out among the Powers natives?"

She nodded. "He said he wanted to be able to hold my hand."

"Are you fucking insane, Harper," Kyle yelled, "Go now."

"Where," she asked.

"The farm, now, I'll work for you, Clora loves me, I'll even shake my ass for her."

Clora did love when a man danced for her. "You don't have an ass."

"She never minded before, go, do you need condoms?"

"No," she squealed. "I'm not...no...I—"

"You're so easy, now, go get your man. Maybe stop at the grocery store, get something to make dinner, some candles, make it all romancy and shit."

Kyle didn't give her a chance to refuse as he jumped from the couch, grabbed her hands, and dragged her to the counter. He shoved her purse in her hands, then led her to the door shoving her out onto the sidewalk.

"I want details, don't disappoint me!"

The door closed in her face, and she stared at it for a few minutes before her brain started formulating all the cons and none of the positives. She wanted more than to be afraid of everything. This required a leap of faith, but did she still have any left? Only one way to find out, she'd survived as much physical pain as a human could take, and she'd survived. She'd survive a rejection too.

She walked back to her apartment to get her car and go to the store, she wasn't the greatest cook, but she could come up with something edible—hopefully.

She adjusted her purse strap on her shoulder as she walked into the alley. She reached into her bag and dug out her keys as she began to ascend the steps. Fire burned along her scalp as brutal hands fisted in her hair. Her scream ceased as her face smashed into the wooden wall of the stairwell.

"No," she whimpered as the too familiar body pressed full-length to her back.

"No, you want to tell me no, freak. When the fuck have you told me no?"

The cool steel tip of a knife skimmed her leg from knee to hip. She sunk her teeth into her lower lip to keep from screaming. She wanted to yell for help—to fight. The stench of whiskey and body odor assaulted her nose.

She cried silently as she listened to the fabric of her dress split under the pressure of his knife. Her flesh gave as wet warmth of blood cascaded down her leg.

"You think you're so beautiful, don't you, you're nothing, and I'll make you even fucking uglier before I'm done."

She once again closed her eyes, and as always, she prayed to whatever deity she no longer believed in that this would be the last time. She couldn't suppress the next scream as her cheek earned the same fate as her thigh. As her vision faded, she tasted blood and lost herself to the pain.

8 Harper Wasn't Going Anywhere, but Home with Him

Sheriff Camden Pelter was about to lose teeth, Gideon didn't have a temper, but the Sheriff was pissing him off. Two hours ago, a phone call woke him from sleep. The only two words he remembered were Harper and hospital, he had made it to town in record time. They'd sedated Harper when she'd arrived.

He held her hand gently and stroked her soft, warm skin. Every inch of her porcelain skin was covered with bruises or bandages.

"Mr. Jane, your fiancée—"

He glanced at Cam to find the light skinned black man shaking his head, but thankfully Cam stayed silent. It was the only way they'd allowed him to stay in her room.

"We'll be reducing her meds in order to let her wake up."

"What are her injuries?"

"Multiple lacerations. We have a plastic surgeon who took care of the wound on her cheek. He assures us he minimized the chances of scarring—"

"I don't care about scarring, I just want her to be okay." He didn't mean for it to come out as harshly as it did, but he was pissed, Bill shouldn't have gotten anywhere near Harper.

"Yes, sir, sorry. She should be coming around soon. Just keep her calm. The attack was savage, but she didn't sustain significant damage. I'll leave you to spend time with her. She'll spend the night here for observation, but she should be released in the morning, barring any complications."

He nodded and turned back to Harper, he raised his hand and stroked her soft hair.

"You're not going to go all Alpha like the rest of the Crews and not let me get a statement, right?"

"That's up to her whether she wants to talk to you or not. She'll be going home with me when she's released, you can find her at the farm."

"Shouldn't you ask her first?"

"You can find her at the farm."

He was done talking.

"Call me when she wakes up."

Thankfully Cam left without busting his balls further.

He still remembered the panic in Twitch's voice when he'd answered the phone. Crave's muffled voice as the big man tried to calm his husband. He hadn't been able to think passed the point of getting to her. He hadn't known Harper long, but he couldn't imagine not having a chance at earning her trust—to just have a chance of making her his. It was quick, probably insanely so, but he wanted to get to know her and needed her happy.

She'd probably fight him on it, but he knew a stay at the farm would be good for her.

A knock on the door caused him to turn, and a tall, slender man stepped inside.

"You must be Gideon, I'm Kyle, Harper's best friend."

"Yeah, everyone calls me—"

"Ghost, Harper said she prefers Gideon, though."

She tended to call him Ghost when they were together.

"I waited for the Sheriff to leave before I came in."

He turned back to Harper, and Kyle stopped on the other side of the bed.

"I shouldn't have sent her home."

"What do you mean?"

"I gave her this whole speech about taking a chance on you. Told her to head out to your place, maybe make you dinner. If—"

"I think the bastard would've gotten her one way or another."

"She's in denial, we all knew about him. A year ago, I made her promise not to harm herself after her last suicide attempt. It just made her find someone who could hurt her."

"What?"

"To punish herself for what she couldn't change. I think it's been going on a lot longer than a year, but I have a feeling it just got worse since I made her make that promise to me."

He studied the man as he spoke; watched the misery twist Kyle's handsome features.

"I always knew Harper was different, so did my parents, it's why we kept her so close over the years. My parents said she needed a loving home. Her parents were indifferent, then cruel when Harper finally figured out who she was. I just wanted her happy and the way she looked when she talked about you, I just got excited about her finding someone.

"I've tried to set her up on dates. For a while, I thought her and Joker had a thing going, but quickly decided that wouldn't be a good match."

He had to agree, Joker was abrasive and leaned toward violence. He knew Joker would never put his hands on Harper, but they...no, Harper was his, he just had to prove it.

"Then she told me she took a nap with you, I might have lost my head a bit. She said she slept and that rarely happens. I've lost count of the times she'd sit at the kitchen table, and we'd talk until it was time for us to go to work."

The afternoon she'd tucked herself against him, he hadn't slept, but he'd watched her. The way her long, light lashes fanned her cheeks, the way her makeup barely covered the dark circles under her eyes. His body had reacted to her closeness—the first time in years he'd wanted anyone. She seemed so delicate compared to him. He'd never analyzed what attracted him to someone before. Joe had been tall and broad, some would say the man was physically perfect.

He'd looked at women before, tall, short, thin and full-figured, dark and light, and he'd never questioned it. Okay, maybe in his teens when we'd figured out he was bisexual and knew how his parents felt about it, seeing their response to Gregory coming out. He'd wished they'd been more like his aunt and uncle, who hadn't thought twice about accepting Gregory or him later when he'd told them he was bi. Maybe he'd wished to be so-called normal, but it hadn't lasted long.

"She'll be fine, Harper will come stay out at the farm for a while, just until she gets better."

"I think she'll like that. She always," Kyle paused as a barely concealed sob caught in his throat.

"She always what?"

"Oh, when we were kids, I think she was eleven at the time, she told me her dream. Man, I gave her shit about it growing up."

He didn't want to pry, but he was curious as to what Harper wanted. "What was her dream?"

"Oh, she'll kill me for this, but…" Kyle grinned and pulled up a chair. "Prince Charming, a house in the middle of nowhere, maybe a pet or two running around, and she wanted to have kids."

"Kids?"

"Yeah, kind of surprised me, with the way she grew up, the whole happily ever after didn't seem like something she knew much about. Well, except for my parents."

"It's a good dream."

"I hope she gets it one day. After all the shit she's been through, she deserves it."

"She does."

"I shouldn't—"

"Don't blame yourself."

"I do, though. Harper has always been stubborn."

"Not a bad quality."

"Not always. I talked to Clora, and she told me to assure Harper that the store is covered and to take all the time she needs."

He'd reached his limit of interaction, and thankfully Kyle didn't seem to mind his lapse into silence. He absently traced the pale pink scars on the inside of her wrist, horizontal and vertical. He glanced at the opposite one and found corresponding marks. The scars made him curious about what other marks her body bore. How else she may have punished herself for something she couldn't change.

Harper began to whimper, and he raised his hand to tenderly soothe her, he watched the rapid movements of her eyes beneath her closed lids. She instantly calmed and whispered his name, he smiled as he lifted her hand and brushed his lips across her knuckles.

"Shh, just sleep, everything is okay."

She relaxed and drifted back into a restful sleep.

"I was right."

"Right," he asked.

"You're perfect for her."

He wasn't so sure about that, he'd try to be what she needed. Only time would tell, but if he was anything, he was patient.

9 Harper Couldn't Just Lie Here

The scent of some rich soup drifted up from the kitchen, and she'd stopped pretending an hour ago that she was interested in the book she'd been reading for the last two hours. Gideon hadn't let her out of bed since he'd brought her home five days before. But she couldn't just lie there anymore. She wasn't used to sitting around and doing nothing.

Gideon had other ideas though. It was becoming routine because the man loved to argue with her. At first, she'd shied away from conflict, yet she strangely enjoyed arguing with Gideon. The distraction was also needed. Bill's latest attack, the things he'd said—she relived them in her nightmares.

She had to go through every detail with Camden. It was the first time she had ever filed a report. Unfortunately, Bill was nowhere to be found. That didn't mean he didn't lurk and wait for the next opportunity.

She grabbed the heavy quilt and threw it off her legs, then she eased from the bed. The healing wound on her thigh pulled uncomfortably, but she stepped gingerly. It was guaranteed Gideon would fuss about her being up. She'd take it to be out of bed for a bit.

Their first fight was about Gideon giving up his room to her. She felt guilty about it, although his bed was comfortable, and she might have relished spreading out in a King-sized bed even on a temporary basis. She fisted her hands in her cotton gown and tiptoed down the steps to the kitchen. A quick peek around the corner revealed the kitchen was empty.

She slipped into the room and strode toward the fridge. She still found it odd that she had permission to make herself at home. Her reflection in the stainless-steel door caused her to avert her gaze. The scars weren't as bad as they could've or should've been, and she hadn't quite processed it yet.

On her list of important issues, her looks were low on it. She avoided attention because most of the time the attention she received wasn't favorable. It normally preceded pain and humiliation.

She roughly shook her head and pulled open the fridge door. She refrained from a silly happy dance at sports bottles of Gideon's iced tea with peaches and mint muddled in the bottom.

"Why are you out of bed?"

She squeaked as she turned to find Gideon standing in the doorway.

"Um, I—"

"I told you to call me if you needed anything."

"You're working. I didn't want to—"

"If you say you didn't want to bother me, we're going to have another disagreement."

"If I'd known you were a dictator I would've gone back to my place."

"No, you wouldn't have, because I said you were coming to stay with me. And I assure you I'm nowhere near dictator status."

"I beg to differ."

"You're not going to change the subject, you should be resting."

"I've been resting for almost two weeks, and I'm tired of it, I'm fine. My stitches are out. The bruises are fading, I'm sure I can go home."

They'd kept her in the hospital for almost a week before they'd freed her to return home. Gideon's house wasn't where she'd expected him to take her. At first, it was odd to take up residence, even temporarily, on the farm, but she had to admit the last five days were amazing. It felt like home there, yet she didn't want to admit it.

"Until they find Bill, you're staying here. Now, since that's over—"

"It's not over."

"Yes, it is. Now come out on the porch, I have a present for you."

"Pre...present?" No one ever got her a present before except for Kyle, Clora, and a few members of the Crews. Gideon had given her flowers.

He turned, bowed and motioned toward the door.

She closed the fridge and hugged the sports bottle to her chest—her steps hesitant.

"Come on, honey, I'm sure you'll like your surprise. You want me to go first?"

"I'm sorry."

"Don't apologize, I'll do this as fast or as slow as you need, I want your trust and I know I haven't earned it yet."

"I'm—"

"Quit saying you're sorry, there's nothing for you to apologize for." Gideon stepped outside. "I had a friend call me this morning while I was in the fields and asked me a favor."

"Oh."

"You can pick one."

"Pick one, what—"

Gideon moved to the side, and her eyes widened at the cardboard box filled with the tiniest puppies she'd ever seen. There were only two, and each looked like it would fit perfectly in the palms of her hands. She barely noticed when he took her drink, and she eased down to kneel beside the box. She started to reach for them but hesitated.

"Go on, you can pick them up. They'll need to be bottle fed for another month."

"Where?"

"The local vet and his husband run a rescue, they shut down a puppy mill. These were the only two that weren't ready to be put up for adoption. Jared thought since I run my own business I'd have the time for them. So I agreed to foster them."

She glanced at him as he sat on the porch beside her.

"I saw them and thought you might want one."

"Can't I have them both," she asked and cringed.

"If that's what you want. I'll let him know. He brought everything we'll need. He said they're some kind of teacup Yorkie/Maltese mix. Specially bred to be tiny. The rest of their litter mates didn't make it. The mother appeared too young and exhausted, it didn't look like she was nursing them. The condition the kennels were in was the worst he'd ever seen. They've been in the clinic for about a week."

"So they won't get much bigger?"

They were so cute and tiny, she rubbed the tops of their heads with her fingertips. She refused to look at Gideon as she tried to blink away tears.

"Harper," he softly said her name, then his fingers stroked her scarred cheek, and his thumb traced the fringe of her wet lashes.

"Thank you."

"You're welcome."

"I want Joker to have one of them."

"Really, I don't know if a micro dog is exactly Joker's style."

She snorted at the amusement in his voice. It probably wasn't, but her friend was way too reclusive. He needed something of his own. Something to focus on other than his demons.

"I have a key to his place, we'll leave it, her, him?"

"Her, they're both girls."

"We'll sneak her in and leave her with a bow."

"Sneaky."

She gently reached into the box and lifted both brown and black puppies, cradling them to her chest.

"Names?"

"I don't know, I've never gotten to name anything before."

"No hurry, you'll figure something out."

"Why are you so nice to me?"

"That's a question I'm only going to answer once, come here."

She nearly dropped her presents when he patted his lap. Did she even dare?

"Do you trust me," Gideon asked. "Even a little?"

"Yes."

"Then come sit on my lap, I won't hold you, you're free to get up at any time. I just want you close while I answer why I'm nice to you. You can even hold on to your new babies."

She nodded as she carefully got to her knees and moved close to Gideon until she could sit sideways on his lap. She buried her face in soft fur and waited. Gideon's stomach was soft against her ribs and hip. His scent was rich earth, sweat, and the incense he always seemed to burn. His beard strangely soft against her neck.

He kept his word, he didn't trap her in his arms. Instead, his right arm laid casually over her thighs and his left loosely wrapped around her. Gideon's large hand rested on her left hip.

"Now, you wanted to know why I'm being nice to you."

She nodded causing his mustache and firm, yet soft lips to brush the still tender scar on her cheek. Harper forced herself not to shy away from the caress. It seemed an inadvertent act. She'd come to rely on her gut instinct when it came to situations where it might prove dangerous for her, but in that instance, she didn't feel the need to flee. She oddly wanted to get closer like she had the day they'd napped, and he'd held her.

"I think I've mentioned it before, I'd like to take you on a date. Get to know you. You're beautiful and sweet, even when you're being stubborn."

"I'm not stubborn."

"We'll leave that as another point of contention."

The corners of her mouth twitched. She really didn't understand her level of ease with Gideon. She lowered the sleeping puppies to her lap and gave into her desire to lean against Gideon, resting her head on his shoulder.

She nibbled nervously on her bottom lip as Gideon's fingertips drew circles on her hip. The strangeness of the gentle touch caused tingles to travel over her skin. She almost crossed her arms over her chest when her nipples beaded against the cotton of her gown. A lifetime of self-preservation urged her to conceal the awakening of her long-dormant libido; she wanted to flee. Although she didn't want to listen to it, she wanted to savor and analyze.

Gideon shifted until he could lean back against the wall of the enclosed porch and rearranged her on his lap.

"So, we have something we need to discuss."

She stiffened. "I don't want to talk about the attack."

"We're in charge of two toddlers and an infant this coming weekend."

"But we have puppies."

"Yes, but everyone arranged for Psycho and Ben to go away for their anniversary. Bernie and Stacey needed a break too."

"With Psy gone, it's all hands on at Brawlers."

"Yes, so, want to be my co-babysitter for a weekend?"

"You're in charge of heating puppy and baby bottles."

"You're in charge of dia—"

"To that, I don't agree, Mr. Jane, that's where the co-babysitter relationship comes into play, we share the horror of diapers."

"Fair enough, Ms. Sage."

He gave her a light squeeze. Gideon was always gentle with her. He claimed she was sweet but he was, and it caused her to wish for things long forgotten. Silly dreams she had always kept to herself. She wanted to believe Gideon was genuine. Craved for the secrets she had decided long ago were unattainable. Maybe she'd finally earned her chance for something more than pain and humiliation.

10 Dangerous Thoughts, Mr. Jane

Two hours ago, he had walked into the cutest sight he had ever seen. He'd found Harper curled up asleep in his bed surrounded by babies and puppies. Instead of waking them he'd slipped from the room and left them there. Gideon had almost given in to the desire lay down behind her—hold her again.

She'd lived there a couple of weeks, and he looked forward to coming home each night. Harper even made a habit of spending some afternoons in the greenhouse with him. Their friends were strangely absent since he'd brought her home. If they were anything, they had reached Matchmaker: Professional status over the years. He'd heard all the stories the Crews loved to share.

"Why didn't you wake me when you got home?"

He glanced up from his laptop and smiled at Harper. Her hair was tangled around her face and shoulders, her beautiful eyes bright and sleepy. Harper lifted her arms, and she pushed her slender fingers through the dark blonde strands, attempting to work out the knots.

"You needed rest, you've been home with the kids all afternoon."

"Gideon, I'm not used to sitting around and doing nothing, it's all you've let me do since I got here."

"Too much," he asked with a smile.

"Yes, and you don't appear very repentant."

"I'm not."

His smile widened as she threw her hands up in the air and pivoted on her bare toes, then exited his office. He pushed up from his chair and went in pursuit of his sulking Harper. No one would think it, but she had a temper he found extremely sexy. When they'd had their first argument, he prepared himself to back off at the first sign of apprehension. It hadn't come, her cheeks had turned pink, and her eyes flashed with indignation.

He'd made a habit of riling her up since. The quicker she realized he wouldn't ever lash out at her in anger, the sooner she'd realize she could trust him. Besides she was cute as fuck when she was in a snit.

Pots and pans clanged, cabinets slammed, and he leaned his shoulder against the door frame. Her long dress whipped around her legs.

"You're cute when you're mad."

She huffed but ignored him.

He pushed away from the jamb and strode across the room, and he placed his hands on her slender hips. Gently he turned her to face him. He wrapped his hands around her sides and lifted her, settling her on the counter.

Her eyes were wide, and her lips parted as she stared at him. Pink highlighted her high cheekbones. Her breathing increased, but he didn't sense fear.

"May I kiss you," he asked.

He resisted the allure of her pale pink lips for weeks. The farthest he'd gone were touches, fleeting moments to get her used to him. He kept it innocent and non-threatening.

"Why...wh..."

"The first night you were here, when I dropped you off, I wanted to kiss you." He rested his hands flat on the counter beside her thighs. "You were skittish around me, I didn't—"

"I've never—"

Harper paused and looked down at her lap, he wanted to see her eyes when she talked. He needed to be able to read the emotions in her gaze, lifting his left hand he nudged her pointed chin until she looked at him.

"Talk to me, baby, this isn't going to work if I don't know how you feel or what you want."

"No one has ever wanted to kiss me before."

He couldn't believe no one had ever wanted to taste her before. The first time he'd seen her at the bookstore and her lush mouth curved into a small smile, he'd barely thought of anything else. He wouldn't lie to himself, he wanted her in his bed, but first, he needed to earn her trust.

Gideon cupped her face in his palms, his thumbs teased the corners of her mouth. Her lips trembled under the tender stroke of his thumbs. Her breaths quick, sharp puffs of air.

"Do you want me to stop? You'll always have a choice with me, Harper, a single no is all it'll take."

"You won't be mad at me," she asked as her eyes closed.

"No, don't close your eyes." He waited patiently until she looked at him. "You'll never have to worry about me being mad about something as stupid as you telling me no. So, may I kiss you?"

He watched her gaze fall to his mouth, then return to his eyes, repeating the motions. He watched the silent battle playing out. Thankfully he still didn't see fear only hesitancy. He tried to pretend it didn't hurt, but her past colored her every decision—every move she made. That wasn't what he wanted.

"Y...yes."

It was all he needed to hear, but he still didn't rush. He had waited too long, and it was her first kiss. He slightly bent forward so as not to nudge her thighs apart. No matter how much he wanted to feel her pressed completely against him, he would only do so if she asked. He didn't take his eyes away from hers as he tugged at her bottom lip with the pads of his thumbs and gently brushed a kiss to the corners of her mouth, brushing the plump curve on each side to side movement.

Her cool fingers circled his wrists, her short nails pricked his skin, and he deepened the kiss. She tilted her head and leaned into the gentle caresses. He nearly groaned as she let out the most beautiful little whimper. She tasted of peaches and mint. The smoky scent of his favorite incense infused her skin, hair, and clothes. Her skin was silky under the pads of his fingers and palms.

Harper was perfection, and he wanted more. He only retreated enough to speak.

"Let me closer, please?" He'd beg her if it was what she needed.

She didn't make him wait long, Harper parted her thighs, and he slipped between them. He dropped his arms to wrap them around her and tugged her flush to him. Her small breasts with their hardened tips flattened to his upper abs. She was warm and soft, he couldn't get over how delicate she felt in his arms.

He didn't tug her hips to the edge of the counter. He kept their lower bodies separated. Her lips quivered as they tentatively touched his. He let Harper have control. Whatever happened between them would always be at her pace.

The tip of her tongue traced his lips. She shook, retreated and advanced, as she chastely kissed him, but he had never felt anything as right.

She jerked back, and he cringed as he heard the back of her head hit the cabinets. He lifted his hands to massage the spot as heat bloomed in her cheeks turning her pale skin bright red.

"Are you okay," he asked.

"Yes, I'm so—"

"Nothing to be embarrassed about. Do you need ice?"

"No, I've had worse."

"I don't like hearing that."

"I can't change my past."

"I don't want you to. Why don't I go check on the kids and give you a minute?"

"Okay."

He gave her a quick kiss before he forced himself away from her. Harper quickly pushed her dress down over her slender legs until it once again covered her to her ankles, then she nervously smoothed the wild waves of her hair.

He took a deep breath as he turned and strode to the stairs, ascended to find Gunner and Rage gently petting the puppies. Sawyer was laid between them.

"Y'all want to help with dinner?"

They nodded in unison but never looked away from the still unnamed puppies. He quickly slipped on the black and white tie-dyed sling and carefully picked up Sawyer to settle the still sleeping baby inside. He showed the twins how to place the dogs in a basket.

Strange and dangerous thoughts started to form in his head. What would a life with Harper be like? Did she think about a family one day?

He shook his head and attempted to rid himself of visions of more than what he had now with Harper. Gideon sat on the edge of the bed, and the twins giggled as they got him in a choke hold. He chuckled as he stood with them dangling and went to rejoin Harper in the kitchen.

Gunner and Rage probably needed a snack, it was time for the puppies next bottle, and Sawyer would probably be awake soon. He was going to enjoy his time with his nephews and Harper. He knew he couldn't keep her there forever, and when the threat of Bill was out of the way, she would want to go home. Until then, he'd savor every minute and each smile she gifted him.

11 What Was She Going to Do?

Night lights illuminated Gideon's bedroom, Gunner and Rage were asleep in the playpen. Sawyer snuffled in his sleep from the bassinet beside the bed. She knew Sawyer normally co-slept with Stacey and Bernie, but she was terrified she would roll over on him. The puppies were curled up in a box with blankets and a heating pad. Everyone was settled in for the night, and she was pacing.

She was mortified about how she'd reacted to the kiss. She twisted a lock of her hair around her finger and tugged until her scalp stung. The slight pain didn't help, she wanted—needed more, but she wouldn't do it. She roughly twisted her hair up and secured it with a tie from around her wrist.

"Want to talk about it?"

She spun to find Gideon framed in the doorway and then dropped her gaze, he was shirtless with his chest and rounded stomach covered in thick, red hair catching her gaze.

What was she going to do? All she could remember was the kisses. She'd loved the feel of his mustache and beard, the warmth of his big body. He was solid and made her feel safe, her body had responded, and she hadn't known how to handle it. She didn't understand pleasure. It was foreign and terrifying. No one had ever touched her like Gideon had.

He'd held her in his strong arms, wanted to be closer to her and she wanted more but hadn't known what to do. She didn't want him to think she was stupid or pathetic.

"I don't know what to say."

"What's on your mind?"

"Do you think I'm stupid or pathetic?"

"Never," he shouted, but when he spoke next, his voice was barely above a whisper. "You're neither of those things."

"I'm twenty-nine, and I'm...I should've—"

"Grab the baby monitor and come with me, I'll make you hot chocolate."

She nodded, grabbed the monitor, and followed him down to the kitchen. Gideon only turned on the hood light over the stove. She watched him move around and gather what he needed.

"Don't you have to be up early?"

He patted the counter next to the stove.

"Have a seat here. I work for myself, and I really don't have much to do on the weekends."

She approached him and let him lift her onto the counter. He had done it earlier too, and while she had waited for the terror to overtake her, it hadn't come. She loved when he touched her. Fleeting caresses she could almost pretend didn't happen. And as brief as they were, they made her feel wanted—needed.

His damp hair curled around his ears and at his nape. She fisted her hands to keep herself from reaching out. It was almost embarrassing how much she loved his scent. She inhaled through her nose and closed her eyes as she let out a sigh. It didn't matter if he had just come in from working or after a shower.

"Now, tell me what's going on in your head."

"I self-harm."

"I noticed the scars while you were in the hospital. Are you feeling the need to?"

She wondered if he'd judge her, look at her with pity in his eyes, and realize just how broken she pretended not to be.

"Yes. I promised Kyle I wouldn't do it anymore, so, I found a loophole."

"Bill?"

She had a moment where she wanted to deny it, but it would be a lie, and he'd know it.

"Yes. I tried to break it off a year ago after my last suicide attempt. Told him not to come around."

"If rumors around town are right, he still makes you his favorite target."

"I knew what would happen, I anticipated the pain. The humiliation. It's not what I wanted yet at the same time it was."

"You turned him into your razor."

She nodded and dropped her gaze to her lap.

"Harper, you don't need the pain."

"I know, but I don't know how to accept pleasure, simple kindness. My secrets, the things I want are the opposite of what I asked—"

"You didn't ask for it, baby."

"Yes, I did. He uses me. Leaves me reminders painted in bruises and pain. Earlier, you…you treated me like I mattered. I didn't know what to do. I've always been the Powers Freak. It was bad enough when they bullied the gay kid, but when I came out as trans and wore my first dress…bought makeup, they beat me." She paused on a sob. "They—"

Gideon was there, his hands gently cupped her cheeks, and kissed away the tears on her cheeks. She couldn't stop her choked cries, and each time a sob broke her breathing, he kissed her. His lips firm and gentle, he whispered words she could barely hear, but the emotion in his voice continued to break her. Each side of her warred with the other, the one that told her she deserved it for not being normal and the other which dreamed of having someone like Gideon to love and accept her. It was a battle without end.

"Baby, you're okay, you're perfect as is. If I could change anything about you, it would be for you to see how amazing you are." Another kiss. "How sweet. So innocent despite the hell you've been through."

She wrapped herself around him, buried her face against his chest, and inhaled. It was home and comfort, caring. The hair teased her skin and nose, she barely resisted turning her head to stroke her cheeks over the thick mat.

"Would you sleep with me instead of in the guest room?"

"Is that what you want?"

She nodded then tilted her head to rest her chin on his chest. His fingers combed through her hair, gently tugging.

"Okay, but it's just sleep, don't try to take advantage of me." His voice was serious, but his eyes shimmered with amusement.

She snorted and then giggled as he kissed the tip of her nose.

"I think I can resist…barely."

"Good girl, still want the hot chocolate or bed?"

"Maybe we should sleep. Gunner and Rage are late sleepers, but Sawyer and the puppies are going to want their bottles soon."

"Power nap it is, just let me put everything away."

She reluctantly released him, but observed him as he moved around the kitchen putting away the milk, sugar, and cocoa. The vanilla went above the coffeemaker where it had taken up residence since she moved in. He'd noticed her putting it in her coffee the first morning.

It was the little things he did that she noticed the most. Those touches. The way he kept her stocked with the peach and mint tea, or a travel mug of coffee beside the bed when she woke up. He picked her flowers. It was all so odd but in a good way. He claimed he wanted to date her. She hadn't dated before. She didn't understand the expectations.

"Quit thinking so hard, baby, it'll all work itself out. We'll do a picnic lunch tomorrow so the kids can wear themselves out running around outside."

"Sounds nice."

He lifted her off the counter and set her on her feet. She almost protested when he turned her and nudged her toward the staircase. Typically, she hated people behind her, but Gideon was different. She held her long gown up as she ascended the steps and quietly entered the bedroom. She checked to make sure everyone was still settled.

Luckily, they were, she really needed a nap before chasing around after them all afternoon.

She crawled onto the left side of the bed and snuggled in under the covers. Before she could give in to her nervousness Gideon was beside her, his body flushed to hers, and his arm cradling her head. She felt the tender kiss to the crown of her head. She closed her eyes, savored his warmth and, for the first time in years, she didn't fight sleep or worry about the nightmares to come.

12 Joker Needed Bail Money...Again

He sat astride his motorcycle and glared up at the Sheriff Department door. Harper was still cackling like a madwoman behind him. He had better things to do at four in the morning than try to get Joker out of a cell. Joker had to stop pushing Pelter.

"It's not funny. I asked you to go to Brawlers, I said you'd be safe, and Joker starts a bar fight because someone may have looked at you sideways."

"That's Joker, he's been watching my back for years, it's sort of a habit he can't break."

"You shouldn't have had to hide behind the bar."

"It wasn't all bad. I got to watch you play, and it was fun hanging out with Stacey and Bernie, Lily and Peaches. I thought I'd feel more out of place but—"

"That's why we asked them to come tonight. Besides, Lily can swing a mean broken beer bottle when the need arises."

"Speaking of Lily, where did she go when the Deputies showed?"

"Little took her out the back."

Little worked for Trenton Security, Linus's company. Surveillance was Little's specialty. There wasn't anything the man couldn't find. The man was also best friends with Lily, Linus and Lucky's mother. Little and Lily were an odd combo, but if nothing else they were great for inappropriate comic relief.

"I hear Damon is actually jealous of his wife's much younger bestie."

He chuckled. "Damon is just giving them shit. Little grew up in foster care, so Damon and Lily treat him like one of the kids. It's good for him. He doesn't get in as much trouble as he used to, I wish I could say the same for Joker."

"Leave him alone, he just has terrible impulse control."

"Terrible, really, that's an understatement."

"Quit being cranky, Pelter will let him out."

"We had to give Sin and Saint bar towels to use as bibs when Pelter came in. I swear those boys were trying to hump Pelter. He didn't look impressed. Actually, he looked even more pissed off."

"The twins are young, they have a little crush."

"I wouldn't call their crush little. I hear the boys are stalking a scanner lately."

Sin and Saint were barely twenty-two, and they were like the opposite sides of a coin. Different as they were carbon copies of each other. They argued constantly, but there was one thing they agreed on, Sheriff Camden Pelter. They hadn't shown interest as far as he knew until that night.

"But that's all they're stalking as far as I know."

"So far."

"I don't even need to ask what you two are doing here, do I?"

Speaking of the object of the twin's obsession. Pelter was a large, powerfully built man, mahogany skinned with pale green eyes. If Pelter smiled he'd be downright gorgeous, but the man mostly lived with a stern expression.

"We came to get Joker."

"I might leave him in the drunk tank until morning."

"Joker isn't drunk," Harper protested.

"I'm going to need to put a plaque on one of the cells he spends so much time in it."

"We were at a bar called Brawlers, can't really be surprised when, oh, I don't know, a brawl breaks out."

He rolled his lips between his teeth to keep from smiling at the thick sarcasm in Harper's voice. She was coming out of her shell. He found it sexy as hell when she got a bit snarky. She appeared more confident than she had a week ago when they talked about Bill and then went to bed.

"Why was I led to believe you were quiet," Pelter asked.

"I am."

"You've been hanging out with the Brawler, Twirled, and Executioner Crews too much."

"I hear you have two very pretty, blond admirers," Harper quipped.

Even under the dim streetlights, he saw Pelter's jaw clench. He didn't figure the man for a homophobe. He assumed Pelter didn't enjoy attention of any kind. The man worked undercover for a majority of his time on the Atlanta Police Force and in the State Patrol. Pelter made a career of blending, so being the focus of much younger men couldn't be easy.

"You're all menaces. If I let him out, you going to make sure he gets home?"

"We'll even tuck him in and give him his favorite blankie."

"Harper," he tried to sound stern, but his laughter ruined it.

"Okay, I'll let him out, but you take him straight home. I'm tired of him taking up residence here."

"It would be easier if you just ignore his proclivities to start fights when he's bored."

"Harper, he needs another damn hobby."

"He's fine, go release him so we can go home."

"Yes, ma'am."

He leaned back against Harper and watched Pelter jog up the steps. Harper laid her head on his shoulder, her breath fanned his neck. Her touches were more frequent recently. He'd also discovered she had a thing for cuddling; he didn't mind in the least. It was one of his favorite activities.

"Do you do this ass crack of dawn stuff often?"

He turned his head to brush a kiss to her forehead.

"Only when we have gigs. The band is more a hobby. Something to do a few weekends a month, our practices are normally just hang out sessions."

"Can I come next time too," she asked.

Her voice all soft and sleepy, he needed to get her home.

"To practice or when we play?"

"Both."

Harper draped her arms around his neck and snuggled into what seemed like her new favorite spot in the curve of his neck and shoulder.

"Okay, you going to make it home?"

"I'm just resting my eyes."

He felt when she relaxed and drifted off, he circled her thighs with his arms and let her nap as he waited for Joker. It wasn't a long wait. He cringed as the door banged open and Joker with his normally lazy pace made his way toward them.

Joker stopped a few feet away.

"Is she drunk," Joker demanded.

"No, she's napping. It's almost five a.m., and we're waiting for you."

"Why? I coulda found my own way home, and I'm sure I can't fit on your ride."

"We just wanted to make sure you got out. You gotta stop this shit, Joker. One day Pelter is gonna stop being friendly."

Joker shrugged and started backing up.

"Here." He dragged Joker's backpack from his saddlebags. "Harper grabbed this."

"Thanks."

As always Joker didn't get within touching distance and took the bag. Joker was one of his best friends, and he still didn't understand or know much about him. Powers was filled with rumors about Joker, but no one ever spoke above a whisper. He'd assumed most of it was bullshit, but if the truth existed in some form within the tales, then Joker had reasons for his touch aversion—for his lack of control.

"Come out for dinner one night this week."

"I'll see what I can do." Which meant *No* in Joker-speak.

"Me and Harper have a little something for you, but you gotta come to dinner."

"Y'all got me something?"

"Harper says you'll love it."

Okay, that was a huge exaggeration, but Harper was right, Joker needed something all his own. Joker lived in a tiny trailer out behind his garage, so one of the micro puppies would be perfect. The man wouldn't tell Harper no. He just wondered if Harper would be able to let go of one of her babies. They were already sporting bows and tiny sweaters. She swore they were freezing to death and they were needed.

His opinion was: whatever made Harper happy.

She'd been nervous about leaving them alone for a night, and luckily, Gregory came over to sit with them.

"Okay, I'll be by mid-week."

"Good enough."

"Better wake her up before you head home."

"I'm awake," Harper muttered.

"Good, I'll kill—"

"Joker, we've talked about this."

"Yes, Harper."

He suppressed a chuckle at Joker's chastised tone. Joker had a soft spot for the ladies of the Crews.

Joker didn't linger, he turned quickly, and headed in the direction of his place.

"Ready to go home?"

"Yes, I want a bed, now." He glanced over his shoulder to make sure she put on her helmet, then he did the same.

"As you wish."

He started his bike, backed up, and pulled out onto the deserted street. It was a Sunday morning, so no one was out and about yet. He relished the feeling of Harper wrapped around him from behind. He was still waiting for the day she would head home, but first, she was going to start back to work. Harper was going a little stir crazy out at the farm.

They'd made a deal he would drop her off and pick her up. Pelter was still having no luck picking Bill up. Even Little and Raul, another one of Linus's guys, couldn't track him down. Until Bill wasn't an issue, Harper agreed to stay with him where she was safe.

Bill was laying low, but the man wouldn't stay quiet long. As much as he hated it, Harper was Bill's favorite target, and he was positive Bill wouldn't give up without striking one last time.

He pushed the disturbing thoughts to the back of his mind and enjoyed his ride home, with Harper behind him.

13 It Was So Good To Be Back at Work

"So, I need details, you've spent weeks with your Gideon. Tell me," Clora begged.

Harper almost laughed at the woman pleading and batting her lashes. Clora hadn't given up on interrogating her since she'd walked in the door thirty minutes before. The older woman had followed her everywhere.

"There's nothing to tell, I'm just glad to be back at work. The farm is great, but Gideon won't let me do anything, except dinner and the battle to let me do that was long and arduous."

She loved that Gideon liked to take care of her. That he worried she was doing too much while she recovered, but she wasn't fragile no matter what anyone thought. He assured her he didn't think of her that way and she believed him.

She sighed as she shelved another section of books. Clora huffed behind her.

"At least give me something, how's the sex?"

"Clora," she squeaked.

"Don't Clora me, young lady, you've been out there weeks with a handsome man."

"That doesn't mean we're," she lowered her voice, "having sex."

"It's not something to be ashamed of, and since you've been out there, I've heard quite a few stories about our Mr. Gideon Jane."

"Oh, and what might those be?"

She felt more than a little frightened to find out. The residents of Powers favorite past time was gossip. She'd been the victim of it a good portion of her life. Gideon was a quiet and private man, she didn't want people picking their—his life apart.

"Okay, I haven't heard anything, it's like the man is a ghost."

"That's why he earned the nickname."

"Yeah, yeah, Twitch and Kyle did share that the man is a perfect gentleman. That he treats you right."

She couldn't deny that, while she loved the perfect gentleman thing, she secretly wished sometimes he wasn't so gentlemanly. That terrified her, though.

She knew what it was to be forced to bend over any available surface. She knew what it was like to cry and beg for it to end. What she knew Gideon would do to her would be far removed to what she was used to—what she had learned to endure.

Her body was going damn haywire, reacting in ways it hadn't since her teens. She hadn't experienced the need to masturbate in years, but now she thought about it, contemplated sex without a sense of foreboding. She didn't know if she could do it. Her own body was her greatest enemy, had been since she realized it didn't reflect who she felt she was.

"Hello, are you listening to me," Clora asked.

"Sorry, I zoned out."

"It's fine, you want me to leave you alone to acclimate to being a working woman again."

"That makes me sound rude."

"No, not rude. You've had some major changes in the last month or so. It's not rude to need time to reevaluate."

"That's putting it lightly."

"I'm going to get lunch, I'll be back in an hour or so. Do you need anything?"

"No, Gideon made me lunch, but when you get back, I'll probably walk over to see Ben and get coffee."

"See you soon."

Clora kissed her cheek and left.

She let out a sigh of relief and felt like a bit of a bitch for doing it. Clora had in some ways been her rock over the years, as much as Kyle. She just wasn't used to all the questions about Gideon and her. A man in her life that wanted to be seen with her on a date was difficult to process.

Clearing her mind, she finished shelving all the books in record time. She knew every inch of Nightingale, memorized every book and section over the years. She parked the cart in the storeroom and quickly took care of the dusting.

The cleaning was pretty minimal except for taking care of the leftover cookies and pastries, coffee and tea toward the end of the night. She made a cup of coffee, boxed the leftovers, along with a few dollars and placed them out on the back stoop. An elderly man who lived on the edge of town came by each night. She couldn't say he was homeless, but the house he lived in was falling down more every month. All she knew was he didn't have anyone, and she'd caught him outside Heidi's Diner several times just staring in.

She walked out back one night a year ago to throw away the trash and found him waiting near the dumpster Nightingale and Ben's bakery, Decadence, shared. She had ignored his embarrassment, but the next night she'd started leaving him coffee and sweets. It wasn't much, but it was something she could do. She almost expected the first offering to be there the next day, but when it wasn't, she figured he was okay with their silent agreement.

She headed up front for tea and a book while she waited for customers. After pulling the sports bottle of tea from her bag, she curled up on one end of the couch and opened her book. As with her attention span lately, she drifted into her head more than she read.

Her mind conjured images of Gideon, embarrassingly they always seemed to linger when her thoughts were of a shirtless Gideon. The man really didn't know what he did to her. She groaned and let her head fall back. Why did she have to wait until she was almost thirty to become sex-obsessed?

She knew she wasn't particularly attractive beneath her clothes. Her body was a roadmap of scar tissue. She'd forgone breast implants, hormones had helped, but she was small chested. The medicine softened her angles, and she'd gained weight. But due to her premature birth, she had always been lithe and short.

Harper didn't mind her penis. She knew others went with sex reassignment surgery, but it was never something she'd seriously considered. She'd found herself when she'd looked into the mirror when she purchased her first dress, and let her hair grow. She hadn't experienced being misgendered by strangers in years.

She still had moments of body dysphoria. Avoided catching her reflection in mirrors. It was like her anxiety or depression, her blonde hair, the dysphoria was just a part of her. If she hated anything about her body, it was the scars, reminders of her not so pretty and happy past. Finally, though it looked like things were looking up. Changing for the better. She felt happier than she had in so long.

Yes, Bill was still a threat, an invisible one since he hadn't made his presence known since his last attack. She realized too late that she unconsciously stroked her marred cheek.

He'd whispered, his alcohol-scented breath telling her how ugly and unlovable she was, how no man would want her. They weren't new—his verbal abuse as brutal as the physical attacks.

In the times Bill left her alone over the years, the brief moments of respite, she loved her life. She had jobs she loved. Friends she adored. A place she could call her own. She was happy and content.

For so long she dreamed about leaving town, finding a place where no one knew her. Maybe find something normal. But even as she thought about it, how could she leave Kyle or Clora, the Crews and Nettie?

The Devil she knew was better than the Devil she didn't, was an easy excuse. She'd lived in Atlanta, went to school there, and she could've stayed even after she'd dropped out. Found a job and disappeared. Yet what had she done? She came home. She'd had the opportunity to start over and hadn't taken it.

Movement in her peripheral caught her attention. Hopefully, it was a customer. She looked up and her mouth curved into a smile, then it fell. Bill stood outside the window. His hair was stringy with grease. His clothes were wrinkled. She grabbed her phone with shaking hands. Gideon and her had talked about a signal if she was in trouble, a text with an H. Terror caused her skin to turn icy and sweat dampened her brow.

Bill smirked. She knew that look, it was always the expression he wore before he hurt her. She typed H into the thread between her and Gideon and waited.

I'm not broken.

I'm not weak.

She mentally repeated the phrases even as her brain called her a liar. How could she be confident one minute and on the verge of running at the same time? She was scared to hit the send button. Years of hiding, trying to be invisible, and all the times law enforcement bullied her out of filing reports. Now she had support, and she didn't know how to take it.

Nausea churned and fear stole her breath, but she tapped send. Gideon would get her help. Her legs trembled and threatened to give out as she rushed for the door. She just turned the lock as Bill stared at her through the glass. His breath fogging it and as he rattled the door, she jumped back. Gideon had been right, she shouldn't have come back to work. She should've waited until they caught Bill.

"You can't fucking hide forever, bitch. How long before your new fuck grows tired of the freak?"

Bill didn't seem to care anymore if anyone knew what happened between them. There could only one reason for that, he planned to carry through with his threats and kill her. A part of her wished for that outcome for so many years, but not anymore, she had a chance for something. She had a chance with Gideon.

She covered her ears and blocked him out. Gideon liked her. Cared about her. He wouldn't—her phone vibrated in her hand. She opened her eyes to find Bill gone and sirens blaring in the distance, growing louder.

She checked her message.

Gideon: *Wren on his way. Be there soon. Be safe.*

Her hands shook as she started to type out a message and squealing tires alerted her Wren was there. The stocky, muscular Deputy was at the door before she had a chance to blink.

"Harper, open up."

She slowly strode toward the door, unlocked it, and Wren pushed it open.

"Are you okay?"

"He didn't get in. He was outside the window. He just...I was probably—"

"Don't say stupid. What he did should never have happened. We're going to make sure it doesn't again."

"Where's Gideon?"

"Probably breaking every traffic law in the books."

"He had so much to do today."

"I'm sure he considers you more important. The Sheriff and the rest of the Deputies are checking the area, Ghost made me promise to stay with you."

"Oh, I don't want to be a bother."

"You're family, Harper, it'll never be a bother. Why don't you have a seat? Ghost will be here soon."

She nodded and made her way back to her spot on the couch. She sat down, but she didn't relax. Her phone was tucked to her chest as she waited for Gideon.

She didn't have to wait long, she heard his truck well before she saw him slam on the brakes out front. She was off the couch and in his arms before he was barely through the front door.

"You should've stayed home."

She leaned back as she glared up at him. As it always was with him, she was safe, and felt no need to censor herself.

"I wanted to come back to work, and we're not arguing about this."

"You might say we're not going to argue, but we are."

Stepping back, she slammed her fists down on the subtle flare of her hips. Wren's laughter had her breaking the staring contest she was having with Gideon.

"When's the big day," Wren asked.

"What?"

"It's like watching Hunter and Linus fight." Hunter and Linus were Wren's husbands. "Why didn't anyone tell us you two were dating? We could've welcomed her to the family and all."

"We're not...not dating, we're friends."

"Keeping it secret, I can respect that. Since Ghost is here, I'll check in with the Sheriff."

Wren disappeared with a grin on his face, and she didn't particularly like it, as if she were some kind of joke.

"He thinks we're dating," she whispered like someone would hear.

He crossed his arms over his wide chest and grinned. "Technically, we're living together."

"We're not—"

"You're in my house. We've gotten puppies. We eat most meals together. I've discovered you're a huge cuddler."

"That doesn't mean we're living together. You only asked me to stay with you because of Bill."

"Actually, I believe I asked you out to the farm several times. So, to be honest, I wanted you there before Bill."

"But he thinks we're dating, I don't want to em—"

"You even finish that, and we'll have a real fight. Why don't we go to Vincent's before we go home?"

She hadn't lived in the same space as Gideon not to pick up on his little quirks. He was trying to distract her. Normally, it made her defensive, but Gideon naturally put her at ease. "Like a date?"

"Not *like* a date, a date."

"Okay."

"So, we have a decision to make."

"And what might that be?"

"Are you finishing out your shift or am I taking you home?"

"I'd like to finish out my first day back."

"Second decision, do I take up residence on the couch or do I go home, and you text me every hour to let me know you're okay?"

"As much as I love your company, I'd like to finish out my day on my own. I'm sure he won't be back."

"Then I require a hug before I leave."

She rolled her eyes as she stepped forward, and he opened his arms. She twined her arms around him and laid her hands flat on his shoulder blades.

"Are you leaving without protesting?"

"I'm mentally protesting. You should be out at the farm until they catch him, but you're also a grown woman who can make her own decisions. You were taking care of yourself long before I came along."

"So, if I said I wanted to go home?"

"I'd throw you in the truck as fast—"

"No, I meant my apartment."

His hold loosened and his shoulders seemed to droop, he didn't let go, but he pulled away.

Harper didn't want to leave, but she'd have to go eventually. The longer she stayed, the less she wanted to go back to her little one room apartment.

"You can move out to the farm. It's not like I don't have the room."

"I'd have to pay rent," she answered without a second thought.

"Why?"

"Gideon."

"Fine, you can pay rent."

"Everything would be fifty-fifty."

"Fine, we'll sit down and discuss it after dinner. What about your apartment?"

"It's a month to month lease, but because I haven't—"

"You can't afford next month's rent?"

"No." It embarrassed her to admit it. She'd taken care of herself, she was never rich, and for a year she had to crash on her best friend's couch, but Harper paid her own way.

"We'll get you moved in this weekend."

Gideon made it sound so easy, and it wasn't. Her pride stung. She allowed herself to get in the position with no easy way out. Harper would've gone back to Kyle's if she had to but she loved the farm. It felt like home.

"Okay."

The shrill ring of the bell had her peeking around Gideon to find Clora rushing inside.

"Harper, why are there...oh, hi."

Harper almost laughed at her boss's wide eyes and speculative stare that bounced between her and Gideon.

"Clora, it's fine, Bill was outside."

"Oh, honey, are you, what am I thinking, of course you're okay. Now, are you going to introduce me?"

"Clora, this is Gideon, Gideon, this is my boss, Clora."

Gideon released her, and she observed them, Clora was a natural born flirt. No man or woman was safe, but Clora kept her outrageous personality under control. She was shocked at not a fluttered lash or innuendo, it was weird.

"Hello, Clora, Harper has told me a lot about you."

"Wish I could say the same, but if you were mine, I'd want to keep you all to myself too."

"Very nice of you to say so. Harper says she wants to finish out her shift."

"Harper, you should go home."

"No, Harper needs to do it, but I'll be back to pick her up for dinner at closing time."

"I won't leave until you get here."

"Very much appreciated."

Gideon turned back to her, and she leaned in when he bent to kiss her forehead.

"You need me, you text, but check in every once in awhile, so I don't worry, okay?"

"You shouldn't worry about me."

"Not happening. You sure I can't talk you into coming home?"

"I need to do this."

"I get it."

She smiled as he brushed another kiss to her forehead. He said goodbye, and she watched him until he got in his truck, then pulled out.

"So, sure there isn't anything you'd like to share?"

"Yes, I'm sure." She walked away with Clora close on her heels.

Maybe she should've gone home with Gideon, but she needed to prove something to herself. She could make it. Life hadn't always gone the way it should have or how she wanted it to, yet today that changed. She'd waited 29 years to find her place, it wouldn't be easy, but she wanted this—wanted Gideon.

All she had to figure out was how to do that.

14 Ghost Really Should be at Home

The music coming from the speakers of Brawlers was damn near deafening, and he was crammed into a booth, blocked from escape by King on one side, and Bull on the other. Two hours ago, Gregory, Twitch, Lucky, and Elijah had arrived at his house, their men not far behind. Harper and him were in the middle of moving her stuff in, then he was physically dragged to King's truck and tossed in back.

He had looked forward to a night of just them. The last few evenings they'd gone through Harper's stuff, decided what could be donated and what she wanted to keep. To say he was surprised by how little she had would be an understatement. It had only taken them two trips to move all the belongings she wanted to keep out to the farm.

He should be at home helping her get settled into her new room. They'd been fighting when everyone showed up. He wanted her to stay in his room, but she was determined to move into one of the guestrooms. It was just a room, but he wanted her to keep sleeping in his room—

his bed. He loved her there, but she'd had other plans, and he respected that.

"You can stay away from your woman for one night, let Harper have some time alone," King's tone was disgusted.

"We were moving her in. I should be—"

"No, you shouldn't, leave her alone and don't even let me catch you texting her."

King was fussing at him like he was a kid, but never even looked away from a grungy looking biker in the corner across the room. He loved King, called the man one of his best friends but the guy had shit taste in bed partners. If King would just admit he had a thing for his former brother-in-law, then King's life would be so much easier.

"Man, don't even think about it," Bull warned King.

"I wasn't thinking anything."

"Where's Mal tonight," Gideon asked.

It was a surefire way to get King's attention. The man's favorite topic was his 3-year-old son, Mal. The kid was a mini-version of King.

"Lincoln took him to see his parents for the week."

"Didn't want to go?"

King shrugged his massive shoulders and finally took his attention away from the mistake in the corner.

"The ex-in-laws aren't exactly my biggest fans."

"They can't still blame you because you and Melanie split up. It's not like the two of you were broken up about it. They still got a problem with Lincoln being gay?"

"It's one of those don't ask, don't tell situations."

"That's fucking rough."

"It is what it is, man."

He knew it was more than that. The breakup between King and Melanie was amicable, she was off finishing college. King was raising Mal. He wondered how Lincoln didn't know King had a thing for him. Yes, the situation with dating the ex-brother-in-law would be weird, but they made a cute little family.

There was a feeling in his gut that King played the game of player out of necessity. King picked the worst guys to hook up with, and the man didn't see the same one twice. Lincoln was a science teacher and football coach at the high school. When Lincoln wasn't working, he spent all his time with King and Mal.

"What about you, man, things going good with Harper?"

"Shit, I don't know."

Joker stepped up to the table with a chair and spun it, then straddled it. The look in his eyes wasn't friendly. His so-called friend had made himself scarce since the night Pelter had let him go. Harper was anxious to give the man his gift.

"Don't make me have to hide a body, Ghost. I might like you but I love Harper, I'll take you out without a second fucking thought."

"Thank you for the vote of confidence, Joker."

"Just saying," Joker said with a shrug.

"Joker, lay off, think about it, Ghost is like the perfect man for Harper. He's all sweet and gentlemanly without all those rough edges. He's a nice—"

His groan cut Bull off, and they all laughed.

"Ain't nothing wrong with being the nice guy."

"Nice guy is like the kiss of death."

"Not when it comes to Harper. Also, I'm sure you got some freak tendencies. You just ain't sharing that shit with the class," King stated.

He didn't even attempt to answer. He called these guys his friends and family, but they liked talking about sex way too much for his comfort. It wasn't that he didn't love sex, he did when he was having it. Yet since his break up with Joe, he didn't have any urge to try even the dating thing again much less the sex. That changed when he met Harper, though.

He wanted to date her. And it was quick as hell, he didn't quite know how to process it. He knew what he wanted. The promise he made to himself and Harper was more important than the chance of sex. He had given Harper her first kiss, and from what he understood sex hadn't been much better for her. Screwing up his chance with Harper wasn't an option for him. He wanted her to have the dates and the cuddling, all the kisses she wanted, and if she was ever ready, maybe more.

It wasn't the time yet. First, he had to get her used to him. Make sure she was safe and happy. At that moment, they were friends, he loved that, and when it was time, he'd see how she felt about turning friends into lovers.

The conversation thankfully flowed to safer topics, and he relaxed sipping at his beer. His friends had already drunk their three to his one, how the hell was he supposed to get home? He looked around until he spotted Hunter behind the bar. Hunter signed that he had him covered.

Tank, one of the owners of Brawlers, didn't speak and most of them knew sign language to communicate. He wasn't great, his signing ability was intermediate at best, but he could get by. He nodded his thanks and went back to sipping his drink. He knew getting a ride from Hunter meant he'd be there to last call. It was what it was, nothing he could do about it now, and he wasn't having Harper come out and get him.

"Have you done the date yet?" King asked.

"Fuck, man, he moved her in," Joker spoke up. "He skipped a bunch of shit."

"Yes." He ignored Joker. "We went to Vincent's."

He tried to get her to go out more, but she seemed content to stay home when she wasn't working. She was back to sitting with Crave's mom and Nightingale's during the week. He understood he was worrying too much, yet he couldn't help it while Bill was still lurking out there. Pelter didn't know who was hiding Bill and they were doing a damn good job of it, no sightings at all since the incident at the bookstore.

"Come on, drink your beer and stop zoning out on us."

"I just wished they'd find Bill so Harper could do what she wanted again without looking over her shoulder."

"They'll find him. Powers is too small to stay holed up long."

"True. I'm just impatient to get it over with."

"Want to get rid of her—"

"Joker, don't fucking finish that. She's staying right where she is."

He got it, Joker was hyper-protective of Harper, and as much as he understood that it was still hard to take. One of his best friends didn't see him good enough. Yes, he was insecure, he would admit it to anyone. The six-pack of his dreams was hidden under the roundness of his stomach. It wasn't bad, he kept in shape working the farm, and maybe it had a little jiggle to it, but it didn't bother him. His friends like to call him cuddly, and he guessed he was. Harper liked it, and that's all that mattered. But platonic cuddling wasn't all he wanted. She didn't shy away from his kisses, so that had to be a good thing. She snuggled up to him on the couch.

"Joker, quit fucking being an asshole to Ghost, man, you should be happy a nice guy took an interest in Harper. I caught her smiling to herself the other day. That's some good shit right there. She ain't as uninterested as you think."

He smiled his thanks to Bull. All the hard edges and asshole nature, Bull was a great guy. He treated Gregory like gold. His cousin didn't want for a thing.

"I'm taking it slow. When she's ready, it's her decision."

"What if she says she ain't interested," Joker asked with a hard glare.

"Then I'll live with it."

It was a half-truth, and everyone knew it. To him, they seemed like a couple, they did everything partners would do, except for the physical stuff. That was fine with him. And if they were never anything other than housemates, as long as Harper was happy that's all that mattered to him. She was special and important, and he would do everything within his power to make sure she believed it, even if that meant letting her go to find someone else. It was what it was, Harper was more important than his hormones.

He just hoped when the time came she didn't rip his heart out when she left. Even Joe hadn't succeeded in doing that, but he felt something for Harper he'd only briefly felt for his ex—love.

15 This Isn't Happening

Her reflection in the full-length mirror in the corner of Gideon's room drew her attention. She was still obsessed with Gideon's shower, so she used it even though she was staying in one of the guest rooms. Inhaling deeply, she held her breath, then let the thick towel fall to the hardwood floor. She slammed her lids closed.

"You can do this, Harper, it's your body." She gave herself a pep talk.

She slowly opened her eyes. She rarely studied her body. Yes, it was different than it was the last time she contemplated it. Last time she'd been just starting puberty. She'd been a kid who didn't recognize the form in front of her. Girls in her class were getting breasts. She remembered them whispering with their friends about getting their first bra.

Harper wasn't that lanky kid anymore. She raised her hands, and she paused as they covered shape of her breasts. They just filled her hands. Marla, Kyle's wife, told her on more than one occasion she was jealous. Marla was a tall, large-breasted woman with full curves, the woman told her finding comfortable yet sexy bras was a nightmare.

Her nipples were slightly puffy and dark pink, they'd always been sensitive, but since the hormones, they'd been more so.

She danced her fingertips down her stomach. Tracing the slightly rounded surface. Goosebumps appeared under her ultra-light touch. She had the smallest curve to her stomach, soft and a bit mushy. She'd always kind of liked it. It made her feel softer, and her hips had a subtle curve to them. The weight she'd gained over the years was minimal, but she also went without sometimes to afford her medicine and rent. She gained almost ten pounds since she'd moved out to the farm and even that bit of weight showed.

She smiled to herself as she pinched the bit of softness of her stomach. Her smile fell slightly as her gaze moved lower. Her penis was small, and she had a neatly trimmed nest of blonde curls. She understood who she was had nothing to do with what was between her legs. She was firm, she ached and her nipples beaded.

This was her greatest fear: pleasure. It wasn't as if she didn't think about sex; fantasize about it. She'd done a lot of it since she'd met Gideon. Her friends were open about sex. Lily, Lucky's mother, there wasn't anything that woman wouldn't talk about. It wasn't like she hadn't walked in on her friends a time or two, they took every opportunity to catch a moment alone together. Psycho and Ben were infamous for outside sex.

She'd seen it all, rough and gentle. She walked in on spankings and moments so sweet, the partners peering into each other's eyes as they made love. When it happened, she backed out as quickly as possible, but sometimes the images became burned into her memory. Especially the sweet ones. They'd been in every position, but what she was jealous of the most were the times they were face-to-face.

The few men who had used her never wanted to look at her. Simply bent her over, did their business, and moved on.

She checked the time, Hunter had called her to let her know he'd give Gideon a ride home after Brawlers closed. It was only midnight, she still had a few hours, she could do this.

"Sex is completely natural, Harper, people do it all the time. Shit, now, you're talking to yourself. This is so attractive."

She huffed as she dropped her arms to her sides and stared at herself. Her hair was a mass of tangled waves. Her nipples were hard, she was there with a half-erection, and she was talking to herself. Thank fuck, she was alone.

"Can't do this," she muttered as she leaned over and snatched her towel off the floor and started to wrap it around her.

"Stimulating conversation," Gideon's deep voice came from the doorway.

She squeaked and tried to cover all the essentials with the towel. Her gaze jerked in Gideon's direction and found him looking away from her, his focus on the floor. It didn't hide the fact he was smiling.

"Are you laughing at me," she demanded.

"Naw, to be honest, you're even cuter when you argue with yourself."

"You're an asshole."

She started to back up as soon as the sentence was out of her mouth. Gideon looked up. She had a split second of fear and instantly felt shame when she realized he wasn't angry. His eyes were wide, and his smile was a bit lop-sided.

"Now, when I walked in I was a gentleman and looked away, I alerted you to my presence, and I'm an asshole."

"You're smiling." She sounded more antagonistic than she felt, but she wasn't sure what was going on in his head. It also didn't help she was naked except for a towel with the man she was just about to imagine having sex with while she got herself off. Which was embarrassing enough.

"You make me do that a lot."

"Really?"

Why did he have to do that? Be all sweet. She wasn't used to it, and she didn't know where they stood since she moved in. Did he still want to date her? Was she just his friend now? She grew more confused by the minute.

"Yep."

"What are you doing home so early?"

"Elijah came by to talk to Scary and Tank for a few, I caught a ride home. You might want to cover your ass, the mirror is not giving you much modesty."

"Dammit." She whipped the towel around her hips and held it in place.

"Shit, asshole, and dammit, within ten minutes of each other, that's got to be a record."

"There's nothing wrong with not cursing." Yes, most of the people she knew used fuck like a noun, verb and adjective, she couldn't forget punctuation as well.

"I didn't say there was, and you're being very defensive. So, want to share?"

She lowered her gaze to the floor. "I was wondering what I looked like."

"Looked like?"

"Yeah, if, you know, I was attractive."

"You're beautiful and perfect."

It emboldened some of her self-confidence because she knew Gideon didn't compliment her just to be nice, but he meant it. "I've got scars, and I'm not," she paused.

"Not what," Gideon asked.

"I've always been jealous of curvier women."

"Oh, but that isn't all you were thinking about."

She shot him a glare and almost went to flip him off, but her towel started to slip.

"I was thinking about sex, okay, sex, fuck." She bit her lip and turned back to the mirror.

"Four cuss words, baby, you're on a roll."

"I'll make it five and an obscene gesture if you don't stop."

"You know why I tease you?"

"Because you're secretly an asshole?"

"You're hilarious. No, because you're sexy when you get all indignant and stand up for yourself. Your cheeks turn all pink, and your eyes brighten. I barely resist kissing you every time it happens."

She started to protest when he stepped out of the archway and strode toward the bed. He picked up her gown she'd left there. It was silk and fell to the floor, she'd splurged on it with her last paycheck. The silk the same shade as the first dress she'd bought herself.

He slowly approached her, she observed as he stroked the smooth fabric before handing it to her.

"I'll turn around, and you can get dressed, I'm sure you're getting a little uncomfortable."

Strangely, she wasn't uneasy, but she didn't admit it. She took her gown, and he turned giving her his back. She dropped the towel and pulled the gown over her head, smoothing it over her hips. It fit tighter, she'd gotten her usual size which meant the weight gain showed. It also felt strange on her bare skin. She was normally cotton and occasional lace.

"What were you doing before I came home?"

There was a gruffness in his voice she hadn't noticed before. He cleared his throat and shoved his hands in his pockets. With him turned away from her, she felt a bit braver.

"I haven't studied myself or masturbated in a long time. I've gained weight since I've been here. I love it. I think it's because I'm happy here."

"I want you happy."

"You can turn around."

She crossed her arms over her stomach because she didn't know what to do with them. When he turned, she had to tip her head back to look up at him.

"This is new," he whispered.

He gripped the gown at her waist and gently smoothed the silk between his fingers. Her breath hitched as his touch stroked her skin.

"I bought it before I came home from work Friday. I hadn't bought myself anything in a long time."

"You look…beautiful in it and under it."

"I thought you didn't look."

Large rough hands palmed her jaw and she didn't have time to think before Gideon's mouth was on hers. Her arms went around his neck as she tilted her head. She loved when he kissed her. The quick ones he did when he just passed her in the hall. The ones he brushed to her forehead and lips when they cuddled. But this one was different, more like the one in the kitchen that had given her thoughts she hadn't known how to handle. Unlike last time, his tongue stroked over her lips, nudged them apart, and slipped inside. She arched her upper body fully into his. Her breasts smashed against his chest. The silk of her gown teasing the pointed tips.

She moaned as her feet left the floor and she twined her legs around his waist. At the edge of her mind, she sensed them moving and then her back met the mattress, her head on a pillow. She leaned back and looked up at him, his eyes heated with desire. Oh hell, she'd never seen someone look at her like that before.

"What are we doing?"

"Ever had a good old-fashioned make-out session?"

His mouth, mustache and beard tickled the side of her neck. "N...no." She stuttered as he rested his weight on her. Nervousness tightened her throat as a thick ridge of hard dick pushed into her soft stomach. Involuntarily her legs fell open wider, made more room for him, and he shifted heavier atop her.

"Well, we need to remedy that. You know what to say if I do something you don't like?"

She remained silent and nodded.

He lifted onto his forearms and stared down at her. "No, I need to hear you say it. I want you vocal. If I do anything and you want to stop, what do you say to me, baby?"

"No."

"So, yes or no, baby, tell me what you want?"

"You."

A feral smile spread across his wide mouth, and the backs of his fingers caressed her cheeks. She squirmed at the intensity of his gaze. The emotion in them she couldn't name. He placed small kisses over her face, throat and upper chest. His breath teased the shallow valley of her cleavage. For a minute she became insecure, sensed him start to move lower then his lips were on hers again. He changed tactics with each push of their mouths, soft and slow, deep and rough.

She dug her fingers into the muscles of his cotton covered back. The powerful dance of muscle beneath her hands caused her to knead. The sounds coming from her would've embarrassed her if not for the fact his groans drowned out her labored breathing and whimpers. His hands fisted in her hair, and she arched, rubbing her nipples against his chest.

Damn, they had to slow down. She opened her mouth to say so, but Gideon shifted on top of her and placed his hand on her ribs. His thumb nudged the underside of her breast. His lips, beard, the weight of him, and the strength in his touch made her brain go blank. The way her body shook mortified her. It was too much and not enough at the same time.

She pushed her head back into the pillows as he stroked down her side to her hip, then lower to curve around the back of her thigh. A squeak sounded in her throat as his fingertips dug into her flesh. The skirt of her gown rose higher. The cool air in the room prickled her hot skin.

"Is...is it supposed..." Gideon sucked at her throat. "Oh hell."

Where silk separated his bare hand from her leg, his warm, calloused hands glided along her thigh, gripped her hip in a rough hold. Was this supposed to be happening? Her mind empty except for what Gideon's touch did to her. Her lips wouldn't form the word no even if she wanted it to.

Desperation and desire caused her muscles to tighten as she sharply arched into Gideon. She's fantasized, dreamed of what being aroused would be like but everything she'd conjured in her brain paled in comparison. It was an overload to her senses, frightening and intoxicating at the same time. It was like a free fall with no parachute.

Then it happened, she froze as she realized nothing was between their lower bodies but his jeans. Would he be disgusted by her? She'd never denied being transgender, but he could look at her clothed and see her as a woman. Her nails sinking into his back must have alerted him because he froze. She watched as he lifted his head to look down at her. His face was flushed and shimmered with sweat.

"Hey, easy, it's okay."

He kissed her so gently and with such tenderness that tears formed at the corners of her eyes. Gideon kissed those away too, one eye then the other. He gentled her instead of berating her.

"Tell me what's wrong."

His voice gruff, but—no she didn't want to say loving. It was too close to all the dreams she'd had over the years. The ones she'd held secret. She wanted love; the happily ever after her friends had.

"Did I do something you didn't like?"

"No, it was too...my gown isn't covering..."

To her complete horror, he looked down between them.

"Baby, you do know I saw all of you before you covered up, right?"

"I'm being stupid."

"When is the last time a partner took care of you?"

"Took...oh no, never."

"May I, my clothes stay on, and same rule applies. It only takes you saying no."

"What...what are you doing to do?"

The speed with which he straightened and knelt between her thighs didn't give her time to react. He gripped the thin straps of her gown and pulled them down her arms, working the nightdress down her body until he removed it. He tossed it over the edge of the bed.

She couldn't take her gaze off his face. She waited for his reaction. The moment she caught Gideon adjusting his cock behind his zipper, she couldn't take her attention away from it. Her imagination started to form a picture of what his dick looked like.

Then he leaned over her, his hot breath fanned her nipple. He plumped her breasts in his hands.

"Oh fuck," she groaned as his lips circled the hard peak and sucked.

After that, it was just a blur of indescribable pleasure. His touches, kisses, and bites took her to the edge only to be brought back when he softened and slowed. He found all the spots she hadn't even thought were erogenous zones. When he abandoned her nipples, her hands took the place of his mouth, pinching and tugging. He dipped his tongue into her belly button. She had no time to protest before he took her into his mouth and sucked her thin length. Rode it in shallow thrusts.

She cried out as she orgasmed embarrassingly fast. Her hips jerked up from the bed. Pleasure radiated from outward along her lips, sending a hard shiver over her. She froze as she screamed as it only intensified. She was caught between the need to push him away or pull his mouth closer, closer won. She fisted her hands in his hair, and her thighs gripped his head, he growled, and another intense wave hit her.

She collapsed in a mass of quivering muscles and sweaty skin. She looked down at him from under heavy lids to find his chin resting on her stomach, a small smile on his face. His hands kneaded her thighs.

"Do you…want—"

"Have you ever watched a man get off for you?"

Oh hell, did he…she shook her head. He was once again knelt before her. His t-shirt quickly disappeared, exposed his hairy upper body. He undid his belt and jeans, his hands shook, and he never stopped looking at her. His pale dick appeared, hard and flushed, his length was impressive, but the girth was terrifying. She clenched at the thought of having him inside her.

He wrapped his large hand around his cock and started to stroke. He groaned and trembled, sweat damped his chest hair, but he never took his eyes from her. She watched as he stared at her body. Desire darkened the blueish green of his eyes. When she realized he focused on her breasts, she raised her hands and cupped them, rolled her nipples and pulled. His breathing was loud and rough, he grunted, and she dropped her gaze to take in his quickened pumps as he jacked his dick. It was harder and redder, leaking pre-cum, the hot drops falling to her pubic hair.

"I've imagined this, jerked off to this." He fell forward to brace his hand beside her head. "Since I found you in my field."

His words were slurred and broken by groans. His cock painted wet patterns on her belly. She couldn't resist, she lowered her hands and pushed his out of the way, she circled him with both. He pushed and pulled.

"Tighter, baby, yes."

He lowered his head, he sucked at her nipples again, and she lifted her hips, rubbed against his heavy, furry balls. His thrusts became harder and faster, the power of them rocked her body, and she wanted to come again. The hairiness of his body teased every inch of her that pressed against him.

His skin was silky and hot in her hands, he jerked every time the tip popped through the circle of her fingers.

His mouth slammed onto hers as wet, heat painted her hands and stomach. She used one seed covered hand to rub her slender length. It didn't take long, and her scream was muffled by his tongue teasing hers. She wrapped her arms and legs around him as he tried to roll to the side. She wanted him there. She wasn't ready for him to leave her yet.

"We've gotta get you clean up so we can go to bed."

"I want to stay here."

"Baby, where else would you go?"

"My own room."

"No, Harper, we'll take a shower and then you're going to sleep right here. Nowhere else."

"Really?" A sob broke her question.

He once again kissed her face, the tears from her eyes, and then her mouth.

"There's no fucking way I'd let you sleep anywhere but with me. Thank you."

"For what," she asked.

"Trusting me, letting me see how sexy and beautiful you are, every inch of you and I mean that."

"My body doesn't bother you."

"I love every inch of you. Now, shower, and no clothes when we come to bed."

"I've never slept nude before."

"Another first, come on."

She smiled at the sudden happiness that infused her as he kissed her, then he helped her from the bed. It was still weird to be exposed and naked with someone. It was even weirder that it was after sex. She ordered herself not to question it. Gideon saw her, and he said he loved what she looked like. She wanted to be confident, to be all the things she'd always dreamed of and finally, she felt she could have them.

He released her hand, turned the water on and helped her inside. She watched enraptured as he stripped out of his clothes. Took in the hairiness of his thick thighs and calves, and dark ginger hair to match his chest. She held out her arms as he stepped inside with her. He came to her with a happy smile. She lost herself in his kiss as steamed filled with enclosure. Even as her pessimistic side reared its ugly head, she memorized it all. Good memories for when the bad times returned, but she hoped she wouldn't need them. Because at that moment she felt right and whole, Gideon had given her a place to be safe and happy. It was the best gift she'd ever received, and she wouldn't take it for granted.

16 Did Harper Regret It?

Sun was already streaming through the curtains when he opened his eyes. Shit, he checked the time, and it was almost noon. He never slept that late. He turned to find Harper's spot empty. He ran his hand over the sheets and found them cold. He sat up, threw his legs over the edge of the bed, and grabbed his pajama bottoms. It was Saturday, so that meant Harper didn't have to work, she had to be around there somewhere.

He padded across the room and down the steps, when he stepped into the kitchen he found Harper sitting in front of the sink with a puppy on each thigh. They were making little squeaking sounds as they drank their bottles.

Harper's hair was in a messy bun, and she wore the same gown from last night. It was perfect against her lightly tanned skin. Shit, she had beard burn on her chest and neck, he was too rough with her. Now that the heat was gone, did she regret it? She was so perfect, and he was…him. He shook his head, he wouldn't let Joe back into his head, even if he thought she could probably do better. He was too damn selfish to let her go.

He smiled at the puppies' tiny front legs holding onto Harper's wrists as if she'd think about taking the bottles away.

"It's almost noon, why didn't you wake me?"

She looked up with a smile, but she seemed troubled. Harper had lived there long enough for him to pick up on her moods. He'd feared the morning-after regrets, or maybe he was projecting. When he'd come home to find her naked in his room, he'd barely hung onto his restraint. Weeks, no, months of wanting her hit him, and he'd looked away to allow her her modesty, but he hadn't been able to force himself to leave.

"I tried, but you growled and rolled over. I thought you were a morning person."

He chuckled and strode across the room, he bent to kiss her upturned lips, and she didn't pull away, that was a good sign. He stretched to his full height and started a pot of coffee. As much as Harper loved her coffee, she rarely drank it at home. Iced tea was her thing.

"I like my routine, not crazy about mornings. When I ran my event company, it was a lot of late nights and sleeping until noon."

He pressed the start button and picked up a mug from the dish drain. No matter how many times he told her to use the dishwasher, she insisted on washing them by hand. Said it was a waste for just dishes for the two of them.

"Do you ever think about going back?"

"No. Don't get me wrong, I do like to go visit friends, but haven't been in a while. Would you like to tour the city next time?"

"Me, go with you?"

"Yeah, you can meet my friends and play tourist."

"I'd...I'd like that."

"Then we'll have to plan a trip. Carol's been begging me to visit."

"Your partner?"

"Yeah, she started out as my assistant, then I moved her up to planner. She has a way of making the impossible possible. I should also check in with Dem."

"Dem, you've never mentioned them."

"Demetri Urban. Caterer extraordinaire. Last I heard he was working in his boyfriend's five-star restaurant and hating it."

"Hating it?"

"Don't let the fancy name fool ya, I found him working at his family diner in the Bronx. He's a natural chef, perfect palette, but his first love is comfort food. The man makes a mean mac and cheese, enough to feed an army. His family is ridiculously large."

He turned and slid down to sit on the floor beside Harper. He inhaled and took in the scent of his soap on her skin. His shampoo in her hair. Fuck, he loved when she smelled like him.

"Why do you have to check in on him?"

"The man is all about the positive. He hasn't ever been in a bad mood. If someone isn't laughing, he isn't happy. He's a goof."

"Did you two—"

"No, I love the man as a friend, but he drives me insane. Last time I talked to him, he was talking about breaking up with his boyfriend."

"Oh, bad relationship?"

"Not that I know of, his boyfriend is way too serious all the time. You've seen Dem. The picture on the mantle."

He snorted as she started to laugh as she realized who he was talking about.

"The man with the arm crutches with rainbow streamers and wearing the huge red clown nose."

"That would be Dem. He attached one of those squeeze horns to one of his crutches. We hid that damn thing when he wasn't looking."

He loved her laugh, he knew he had fallen way too quickly for her, but he couldn't regret it. This was all new to her, so he tried to rein in his urge to tell her. Instead, he showed her. He touched her. Complimented her and made sure she knew he appreciated her. He didn't want her to doubt he wanted her and just not in his bed. As much as he wanted to love on her, he didn't want to overwhelm her.

"Harper," he said her name, he needed to ask her about last night.

"I don't regret it if that's what you're thinking."

"I didn't exactly mean for it to go that far."

She didn't answer just took the empty bottles and set them aside, then placed the still unnamed puppies back in their basket.

He leaned back as she suddenly straddled his lap and locked her gaze with his.

"I could've said no, Gideon."

"I know."

"Everybody might think I'm broken, and maybe in some ways I am, but I'm finally finding myself, where I'm happy. I don't know what you want from me though."

He wrapped his arms around her hips and shifted her closer. She relaxed on his lap, and he couldn't help taking in the expanse of her bare, tanned thighs. Neat rows of pale scars marred the insides, she had matching ones on her ribs and hips. Last night he'd tried not to linger on them, but

128

he'd brushed kisses to them, fleeting but in some way wanting to kiss away the pain she'd put herself through. He knew he almost never even met her. A year ago, she'd attempted suicide for the last time. He knew her secrets, she told him the stories as they cuddled or when he'd come to her to wake her from a nightmare.

The fact that he came so close to never being able to hold her—show her she was important to him—hurt, but he knew he was nowhere near the pain she'd gone through over the years.

"I want you here. Happy. Healthy. I want a chance with you. More than friends or roommates."

"I think we kinda went past friends and roommates last night unless you're tacking with benefits on them."

"Okay, I admit, the benefits are amazing." He chuckled as she pushed at his chest and glared at him. "But I'd prefer lovers, partners, to be able to introduce you as the girlfriend, not just friend."

"You want that with me?"

"Of course, maybe I've been too subtle about it."

"I know you've been patient and I appreciate it."

"But?"

"I want to be enough on my own. I've got all these hang-ups. I didn't have a choice about living openly as a transwoman. Everyone knew me before the dresses and the hormones."

"I didn't, yes, I knew when you told me your name who you were. It didn't change anything about my attraction to you. I've been bi for as long as I remember. Why should gender or gender identity change how I feel about someone—feel about you? I want you confident in your own skin and body, independent and happy. I don't want to change you. You be you, I'll be me, this is just us in this relationship. No one other than us has to get it or approve."

"You won't be embarrassed by me?"

"Baby, there is nothing about you that would embarrass me or anyone else."

"So, we're dating?"

"Technically—"

"We're living together, smartass."

"You're sounding like a member of the Crews already."

"I always wanted to belong, to be a part of them. Even when I was a kid, I saw Gib and Peaches, the way they were when Landon was unapologetically out, or Lucky and his high school boyfriend. I wanted that freedom, but I felt..." She paused and sighed.

"You still felt different."

"I looked in the mirror and knew, was positive I was a girl. I was so jealous when the other girls were getting bras or came to school in a new dress. When they were allowed to wear makeup. Kyle's parents let me wear my first dress, and his mom taught me how to do my makeup, they were supportive, but because of who I was, I had to hide."

"No need to hide anymore. The good people outnumber the bad ones in Powers, Pelter won't overlook hate crimes. He took a report, has your back. I understand it'll take awhile for you to find a comfortable medium."

"Strangely, I'd already found it. I just didn't want to accept it. So, I have some news."

"Oh, and what might that be."

"Joker is coming for dinner tonight."

"You ready to give one of them up?"

"One of them reminds me of Joker."

He knew which one she was talking about. One of them had a split ear and a scar that married its nose. It also had a bit of a shitty personality. She made the cutest little growls like she thought she was a hundred pounds and not barely over a pound. "She's a bit of cranky puppy."

"Exactly. I even got her a t-shirt and goggles."

She reached up and grabbed a bag off the counter. When she pulled out the items, he lost it. It had to be custom because it had a flaming skull with the caption *my bite is bigger than my growl* on it. The goggles in question were almost like Joker's welding ones.

"Her outfit for tonight?"

"She needs a bit of an advantage."

"Yes, she does. Grocery run?"

"We definitely need to go. The freezer is getting low on meat. We have like two eggs left."

He watched her with a smile tugging at the corners of his mouth as she picked her phone up from the floor and started making a list. He slipped his hands beneath the soft fabric of her skirt and gripped the lush curves of her ass. He smirked as she fumbled the phone. His dick hardened, and he rubbed her against him.

"I'm trying to concentrate."

"You saying I'm a distraction."

"A really, really good one."

"Fine, grocery shopping first, then some more making out when we get home."

"Fine, if that's what you want."

"I know you're joking, but whatever happens between us is always mutually consensual. I just want to make that clear. I don't care if we're friends or lovers, you always have the right to tell me no."

She nodded, and he kissed her.

"Let's go get ready, you want to shop local or head out to the highway and hit the big grocery store."

"Probably cheaper to take the road trip."

"Alright, let's get moving. Steak and baked potato is all Joker will eat."

"He's so picky, six pancakes, lots of butter, minimal syrup every day for breakfast. Peanut butter sandwich for lunch, dinner meat and potato, no dessert."

Which he found weird, he'd watched Joker stare longingly at Ben's pastry display more times than he could count, but only ever orders a black coffee. He'd heard the story about when Twitch baked Joker a cake the first time, and it ended up splattered against the kitchen wall, Joker had disappeared for days after that. There were strict rules when dealing with Joker. Don't come up behind him. Don't touch him—ever. Don't bring him sweets. He wondered how the man would handle a present. If things went bad, both puppies would stay with them.

"His mom made him a birthday cake before she disappeared on his sixth birthday. She hadn't been able to afford decorating icing, but she had some pink icing leftover from a cake she'd made for a friend's daughter. His dad beat them both, smashed Joker's face into the cake and called him names. Said he had a son, not a daughter."

He didn't know what to say, but it all made sense. He'd seen the whip marks on Joker's lower back when Joker had stripped out of hoodie not long after he'd moved there. He'd pretended he didn't see them and then the stories made the rounds when it was discovered he was friends with Joker. There was no reason to repeat them, it was Joker's business. Joker's pain to share.

"Joker used to talk to me when he'd bring me home from the hospital after Bill's attacks, and he thought I was sleeping. I've never told him I heard every story. Joker deserved to be able to talk them out, even if he thought he was confessing every nightmare to a sleeping woman."

"He'll be fine. He'll love his present. Joker needs something to come home to."

It was all they said when he helped her to her feet, and he got up so they could go get ready for the trip to pick up supplies. They were going through groceries quicker with the two of them.

They'd make dinner for Joker, see if he'd like to crash there so he didn't have to go home to his tiny trailer. Maybe even if Joker said no to the puppy first, an evening around her would make him want to take her home. If not, there was always Harper's option, break into his place and leave it for him. Either way, Joker was getting a friend.

17 Was Joker Actually Smiling?

The dishes were done, dried and put away, leftovers were put into storage containers to go home with Joker. She knew he ate most of his meals at Heidi's Diner. It was home cooking and comfort food, it also got him out of his place for a bit. Joker was as anti-social as they came.

She scooped Joker's puppy up and held its tiny face inches from her own. "Okay, you're about to meet your new Daddy, so we're going to have to have a talk."

Tiny eyes blinked rapidly, long lashes fluttering. For being as cute as it was, the puppy had an evil little personality. Not bad, just a bit on the mischievous side already.

"Be an asshole, be his spirit animal, be an asshole."

She jerked her gaze to the door as she heard laughter and found Gideon filling the doorway, empty beer bottles in his hand. She lowered the puppy and cringed as her face went up in flames.

"I'm going to start keeping a tally of every time you cuss."

"Kiss my ass." She snarled her nose and narrowed her eyes.

"Fuck, that was sexy, we'll definitely do that kissing your ass thing later."

She tried to keep a stern expression on her face, but it fell when he went all Groucho Marx with his waggling, thick brows.

"Stop, I'm trying to prepare the puppy to be Joker's spirit animal."

"I think it already is."

She shook her head as he stepped into the room, threw the bottles in the glass recycling bin and headed for the fridge. He made a detour to kiss her cheek before going to grab more beers. She brought her attention back to the mission at hand and dressed the puppy in her new shirt and secured the goggles around her neck covering the black studded collar. While Tiny, her puppy wore a hot pink one with peace signs on it. Subconsciously she must have known which puppy would be Joker's early on.

"Come on, before Joker decides to sneak out while we're not looking."

"He wouldn't do that, he's on beer six, and he never drives after four," she said as she straightened the shirt and goggles once more. A micro dog fit for a biker.

"Really?"

"Yeah, he's drinking more because he's going to crash here tonight. I changed the sheets on the guest room bed before he got here."

"He's been drinking more than usual lately."

"His birthday is coming up in a few months."

She picked up Joker's puppy from beside the care package she'd already made for Joker to take with him. Puppy milk, a few extra bottles, puppy food, toys, everything Joker would need to start off with. They'd started giving them puppy food softened with milk every other feeding now. Another week, they'd be strictly on regular food. She was looking forward to no more bottles every three to four hours.

"I'll grab Tiny."

She nodded and walked ahead of Gideon and out onto the back porch.

"What the fuck is that," Joker demanded.

"Yours, here." Harper went all in and placed the puppy in his hands, then stepped back.

"What the hell do you mean mine? What the fuck do I want with a rat?"

"It's not a rat, it's a puppy."

"That's not a goddamned dog, that's a fucking ankle biting yipping thing."

"Well, too damn bad, she's yours and needs a name."

"I'm not taking it, Harper."

Joker tried to thrust the puppy back at her, but she held up her hands.

"No, it's yours, you need something that's yours, don't make me fucking cry."

"What the fuck are you cussing for," Joker shouted and turned his attention over her shoulder. "This is your damned fault, she was perfectly sensible before she hooked up with you. Now she's giving me rats!"

Harper glanced at Gideon to find him holding his hands up with Tiny cradled in one and backing away. She rolled her eyes and turned back to Joker.

"It's not a rat, she needs a home, and you need something to come home to, so you're taking her. Now name her," she ordered.

"Why is it wearing clothes?"

"They get a bit shivery, so you'll have to cuddle with her."

"I don't fucking cuddle, Harper."

"Now you do."

She stormed back into the house, grabbing Gideon's shirt as she went and tugged him inside with her. She rushed to the window to stare outside and see if Joker was bonding or trying to hide his puppy and escape.

"What are you doing?"

"I'm watching him to make sure he listens to me."

She noticed Gideon taking the spot beside her at the sink. Tiny cradled in one arm and he wrapped the other around her waist, pulling her to his side.

"What's he doing?"

"He's looking at it like it's going to explode at any second."

"You know he hates routine change, and now you're giving him a micro friend."

"I just want him to have something that makes him happy."

"I know you do, Harper, you just need to give him a few extra minutes to process."

"I am."

She impatiently watched as Joker had a stare down with the dog that barely filled his palm. Joker's lips were moving so she knew he was talking to it or cussing her. She smiled as the puppy lowered her head to her tiny paws, then her little butt rose, and she knew the growling started.

Her eyes widened as an actually smile curved one side of Joker's mouth.

"Oh damn."

"What, what's happening," Gideon asked, and then he was behind her.

"Is Joker smiling?"

"Joker smiling is never a good—"

Joker grabbed the puppy and shoved it into the pocket of his hoodie, with only the puppy's head sticking out, then he disappeared.

"Where is he going?" She lifted on her toes to try and track his movements.

"He isn't going to take it to the woods and leave it, is he?"

"I hope not, I better go—"

Gideon's laughter cut her off, and his chin rested on the top of her head. She was handed Tiny, and Gideon held her to him.

"He's fine, he'll take a walk and process. You know he needs some time alone when he has a decision to make. He would have left her behind if he didn't want to take her."

"Did I do the right thing?" She was suddenly feeling insecure about her belief Joker needed something his own. "I just want him happy."

"He'll be fine, baby."

"Thank you." She sighed and leaned her head back against his chest.

"What are you thanking me for?"

She turned, placed Tiny on the floor, and she waddled off with a disgruntled huff. Harper leaned back far enough to be able to meet Gideon's gaze.

"Everything. You didn't have to bring me here from the hospital. You didn't have to be nice to me or take care of me."

She leaned in and laid her cheek on his chest, and she listened to the strong, steady rhythm of his heartbeat. His fingers drew soothing patterns on her back, and she relaxed against him. Gideon treated her like she'd always wanted to be treated.

"What the fuck is wrong with it," Joker demanded.

She popped her head up to find Joker holding out a whimpering unhappy puppy.

"Is it broken? Did I fucking break it?"

"She wants a bottle."

"Bottle? You gave me a high maintenance rat?"

"She's not high maintenance or a rat."

She poked a laughing Gideon in the ribs, and it only made his guffaws louder. She pushed out of his arms and ignored Joker's complaining and Gideon's amusement as she set Joker up with a bottle. The corners of her mouth twitched as Joker bitched under his breath.

"You going to make yourself useful or just stand around laughing all night?"

"I'm going to check on the orchids that came in today."

"Okay."

Gideon kissed her as he passed and Joker made gagging sounds, so she kicked his shin. Joker had done that all night any time Gideon showed her affection. Which was a lot, so she was surprised Joker hadn't puked yet.

She watched Gideon until he disappeared down the hallway toward the front door.

"You look good, Harper."

She barely heard Joker speak.

"Thank you."

"He treats you good, right? He doesn't..." Joker stopped talking.

She knew what he wanted to know. Did Gideon treat her different? Did he hurt her? She knew every painful and humiliating detail of her best friend's life, even if he didn't know it. How Joker survived amazed her.

"He's gentle with me, Joker, I promise."

"Okay, but if he isn't, you'd tell me? He's my friend, but you're my best friend."

"I promise I'd tell you."

She loved Joker, most people in town probably thought they'd had something going on for years, but Joker's hang-ups were worse than hers. She couldn't remember the last time someone touched him outside the instances where they put him in cuffs and dragged him off to jail.

One second she reassured Joker that Gideon treated her right and the next she was plastered to the kitchen floor with Joker's heavy body on top of hers. That's when her brain registered the sound of gunshots and glass breaking.

"Gideon."

Fear had his name breaking on her lips. Bill was an expert marksman. Was Gideon okay? Was he hurt? Terror and guilt took her throat in a chokehold. She'd brought Bill there; to Gideon's home.

"If he's smart, he's hunkered down."

"He's in the greenhouse, not a lot—"

Before she finished speaking Joker was crawling across the floor, Tiny and Joker's puppy shoved inside a carrier.

"You got a place to hide here?"

"I can go to our room. Gideon's walk-in closet exits to the upstairs hallway."

"Take the carrier, stay low, I'll go save your man's ass. Call Pelter, then Linus."

She sharply nodded her head, she crawled across the floor and pushed the carrier in front of her until she reached the stairs. The enclosed space gave her cover. She ran up the steps with the puppies protesting being jostled. She crouched down to avoid being seen through the floor to ceiling picture windows. She ducked into the closet and slammed the door behind her. She crawled to the back, shielded by Gideon and her clothes.

She put her fingers through the thick wire of the crate door and tried to soothe the puppies. In turn, she tried to take comfort in the warmth and softness of their fur. She pulled her phone from the pocket of her dress and called 9-1-1 and listened to the ringing. She rambled on, talking about everything and nothing. More shots made her jump. An operator picked up, she gave them the information they asked for and requested Pelter.

When they asked her to stay on the line, she hung up and called Linus.

"Trenton," Linus gruff voice came over the line.

"Linus, Bill's here. Shots fired. Joker and Gideon are outside."

"Slow down, Harper, are either of them armed?"

"Joker's a felon, and Gideon doesn't have a gun as far as I know."

"Where are you?"

"In Gideon's closet. There's a hidden exit to the upstairs hallway."

She listened to Linus talking to someone in the background, it sounded like Little and Liv, two members of his team.

"We're headed your way. You stay in the closet. Stay quiet. Stay low."

"But—"

"Honey, we've got your man covered, don't worry. You got the cops on the way?"

"I called and requested Pelter."

"Don't make a sound until you hear one of us calling you."

"O…okay."

She didn't want to hang up, but she had to be quiet, needed to keep the puppies calm. Adrenaline ebbed away, and panic took over. A steel band circled her chest. Her breathing became nothing more than useless gasps for air. She couldn't black out. She wouldn't black out. She was stronger than that. Closing her eyes, she tried to find her happy place, a picture of the fields during a rainstorm started to form. She worked up from the thick mat of grass, rows upon rows of vegetables, and fruit trees. Gideon stood center stage. His ginger hair wet and the smile she liked to think of being all for her curved his mouth.

The pressure of her chest eased, but didn't go away; it was enough, though.

Sirens blared in the distance, there were no more shots since she'd called 9-1-1. It didn't mean Bill wasn't still out there, waiting for more targets. Bill was just like his late uncle, the former Sheriff, except his bigotry was fueled by self-hatred, the fear that people would know what he was. She listened to muffled shouts, she couldn't make out the words, but the emotion in them was rage.

As much as she wanted to run outside and find Gideon, she did as Linus ordered. She closed her eyes tighter and forced herself to wait. Gideon was okay. He had to be. She just needed to wait until it was safe and she could see for herself.

18 This was Supposed to be her Safe Place

Gideon quickly grew tired of the EMTs probing superficial cuts he'd gotten when a few panels of his greenhouse exploded. He'd ducked for cover in time to avoid a bullet, not so much the glass. Unfortunately, Joker took one to the shoulder, and they were threatening to sedate him. Harper was doing her best to calm him down enough for the paramedics to at least take care of it. Joker's touch aversion was making his need to be a patient impossible.

"Man, I'm fine, I don't even need stitches, just knock the shit off," he growled.

He just wanted to get to Harper. She was distracted by her job as Joker's Keeper for the moment, but soon it was going to hit her. He needed to be there when she needed him.

"Percy, take a walk."

He'd never thought he'd be happy to hear Pelter's voice, but right then he'd kiss the man. Okay, maybe not.

"Thanks, Cam."

"What the fuck happened, I can't get any answers while Joker is threatening to break the arm of anybody who touches him. Harper is trying to calm him down, so I can't get a statement."

"I don't know much other than there were gunshots and windows exploded."

"Bill?"

"I can't say for sure, but it's a pretty damn good guess. This was supposed to be Harper's safe place and—"

"Don't start blaming yourself. We'd been waiting for this. Although, I wasn't expecting a shootout."

"Shootout implies we were able to shoot back."

"Yeah, yeah, Linus called a friend of his, we got some guys bringing out some plywood to cover the windows. We didn't know what to do about your greenhouse."

"In the morning, I'll get out and get some new panels. It was only a couple. I got some plastic to cover them. Everything should be fine until then."

He stood, and moved around Pelter and headed in Harper's direction. Pelter walked beside him. Thankfully, the man didn't talk or attempt to interrogate him. He stopped behind her. Normally he'd embrace her and tug her back to him, but after the night they'd had he erred on the side of caution.

"Harper, baby," he said her name and then he had an arm full of Harper. She had her face buried against his neck. Her body shook, and tears were warm against his skin. He held her tighter. He knew it was going to happen and even though her crying broke him, it was the silence with which she cried that hurt the most. He raised his hand

and cupped the back of her head, stroked her soft hair as he let her get it all out.

"Just give me some goddamned tweezers, and I'll take it out my fucking self."

"Quit being a fucking dick, Joker, let them take you in," Bull growled as he appeared next to the gurney.

"Fuck you, man."

"Ghost, we set up Psycho's old trailer for y'all to crash at tonight until we can get everything cleaned up and fixed."

"I appreciate that. Where's Gregory?"

"Putting in supplies for the night. Lily sent out a little medicine if Harper needed it."

"I'm not hearing this," Pelter shook his head and stormed off.

"Knew that would get rid of him. Linus said Bill set up on the Northeast side of your property. Signs of a camp, maybe a few days' worth of trash."

"Any other sign of him?"

"Liv said it looks like he's cleared out. They did a perimeter search, no sign of a vehicle, just some tracks."

"We'll go pack a bag for a night or two."

"Y'all taking Killer with y'all," Joker asked.

Harper's anguish suddenly turned to laughter, and his own lips started twitching. Why he was surprised, he didn't know.

"Who the hell is Killer?"

Someone produced the one-pound Killer and Bull lost it as Joker held the puppy to his chest.

"Don't make fun of my dog. Don't underestimate her, just because she ain't big."

Just then Killer went on the defense and let out the cutest warning growls anyone would ever hear. But what he noticed more was the way Joker gently scratched Killer's back and gave the barest smile.

Bull leaned to the side and whispered, "He's smiling, should we take it away from him?"

"Naw, he's fine. We'll take Killer and Tiny with us don't worry about it. I'm going to take Harper inside, grab some things."

Bull nodded in answer never taking his gaze off Joker and the man's new friend.

He led Harper toward the house. She held tight to him. When they were inside, she pulled him to a stop. He smiled as he looked down at her, and raised his hands to wipe her tear-stained face. She was slightly snotty, and her eyes were red-rimmed from crying, but still beautiful. He opened his mouth to tell her, to say he loved her, but she deserved to hear it when they weren't standing on broken glass with police and paramedics outside, not to mention a whole crude mouthed and foul tempered security team.

"I'm sorry."

"For what?"

"This is all my fault, I brought him out here. Your home wouldn't be ruined if you hadn't have been nice to me."

"You stop that now. It's our home. Windows and everything can be fixed, your safety and happiness is more important than some four walls. We'll go stay out at Bull's place for a few days while we figure out what needs to be done. After that, we'll come home."

"Maybe I should go back to Kyle's or see if I can get my apartment back."

"No, Harper, we knew something would happen, so it's a little more extreme than we probably anticipated. That doesn't mean anything has changed."

"You still want to be with me?"

"Of course, that hasn't changed. Now, what we're going to do is take Bull up on the offer of the trailer. So, go pack a few things, and we'll get going."

She nodded and rose on her toes and gave him a quick kiss before hurrying away.

This might have turned into a step back, and he was going to have to fight against her guilt, but that didn't change the fact he thought she was worth it. They'd catch Bill. He'd make Harper his, and he'd prove all he wanted was her. It wasn't as if he hadn't gone into a relationship with Harper knowing things would be equal parts familiar and different.

He loved Harper, everything about her, and all he wanted was her to be herself. She might not think it, but she was a strong, amazing woman. Surviving in Powers as the only out transwoman took courage and strength she didn't realize she possessed. He saw her and loved her for her.

He hurried off to their room. When they returned home, he'd talk to her about moving her things. He needed more than her presence in their bed. He wanted her to comprehend that this was her home. That they were together. He didn't know if she quite got it yet. He was patient with her, understood this was all new to her. It was new to him too.

If he were honest with himself, his relationship with Joe had existed too long as a youthful crush that turned into routine. What he felt for Harper was stronger—different—and everything he'd always dreamed of when he thought about the perfect partner.

He opened drawers, stuffed a few days' worth of jeans and t-shirts, and essentials into a small duffel bag. He heard

Harper moving around the kitchen, he was sure she was gathering what the puppies needed. Zipping the bag closed, he picked it up and jogged downstairs.

She was moving around the kitchen, and Tiny running around her feet.

"Man, take this thing." Bull held out Killer.

The man acted like it was going to go for his throat. Killer was trying to shake out of his hands. Her tiny body twisted back and forth as she snapped her microscopic teeth.

"How the hell did you find a rat with Joker's personality?"

"She's just fine," Harper said and removed Killer from Bull's huge hands, then set Killer on the floor. "Go play with your sister."

"He didn't want to give her up, but the paramedics wouldn't let him take it. Y'all about ready, Gregory is tearing my phone up wondering are we headed that way yet."

Bull smiled every time he said Gregory's name. The mean and rough man softened at every mention of his husband or when they were together. It was like Bull was two different people, the one with Gregory and the one away from Gregory. It was odd and sometimes disconcerting to see.

"I'm ready. Harper, do you have everything?"

"Yeah."

He watched as she carefully put the puppies into the carrier, grabbed the basket with everything the animals would need, and then slipped her own bag onto her shoulder. She seemed sad and defeated, but she attempted to hide it. It didn't work with him, and they'd talk when they got to Bull's place. He stepped forward and grabbed the carrier.

Harper needed her rest. He nudged her forward, and they followed Bull outside. Gideon talked to Pelter for a few minutes, thanked everyone, and wanted to get somewhere else so he could take care of his woman.

19 She Wasn't a Victim

I'm not a victim, Harper repeated the phrase as she stared into the cloudy mirror of the tiny bathroom. Crazy thoughts kept assailing her. Half-formed plans of running someplace Bill couldn't find her. Hallucinations of turning her mental and emotional pain into a physical reminder. Her eyes were red and dark circles marred the tender skin beneath them.

She'd brought all this on Gideon. This was his reward for caring about her.

That wasn't getting her anywhere, and she could stay in there all night. Gideon had given her space since they'd settled into the trailer an hour ago. Thankfully, they hadn't stayed in the main house too long before he'd made their excuses. She loved the crews, especially Bull and Gregory, but she started to feel suffocated by all the attention.

All she wanted was quiet—to spend time alone with Gideon, but what was she doing instead? Hiding from him.

She still feared when the time would come when he grew tired of her or finally realized she wasn't worth the trouble.

She wouldn't cry, she ordered to herself. She turned off the light and opened the door to find Gideon leaning against the counter. Shit, he was shirtless, his pajama bottoms hung low on his hips, and he looked—damn. How the hell did he do that? One look and she went weak in the knees like some teenage girl with her first crush.

"Now, there is something very wrong with this picture," he whispered.

"What, what's wrong," she asked as she looked down at herself.

She wore her usual long, cotton sleeveless gown. It was what she wore every night, did he not—her mind emptied as he reached forward and picked apart the tiny buttons. Just enough of them to push it off her shoulders and for it to pool around her feet.

"I'd keep you naked all the time if I could."

She turned shy at the compliment and the heat in his gaze as he stared at her. She bit at her bottom lip as she noticed his dick pushed at the thin fabric of his sleep pants. She waited for her usual self-consciousness to take over, to force her to cover up and hide her body. With a jolt, she realized it wasn't there.

She raised her hands and pushed him until he was braced against the counter. His eyes widened as she dropped to her knees, she nipped at the curve of his stomach, and didn't take her gaze off him as she fisted her fingers in the waistband of his pants. She slowly pulled them off, and he stepped out of the legs.

Sitting back on her heels she looked at him, she visually devoured everything inch of him. He was big and solid, she remembered the weight of him and the tease of his body hair against her skin. The perfect roughness of his hands. His scent—she leaned forward and buried her face in his thick bush and inhaled.

He combed his fingers through her hair and held her close. His dick was hard beneath her chin, the tip wet against her throat. She didn't know what to say, her thoughts too chaotic, but she could show him.

She retreated until his cock hovered in front of her mouth, pearls of pre-cum beaded at the slit and she opened her mouth, flicked her tongue out to taste. She moaned as she wrapped her lips around him and sucked him all the way in. The blunt, spongy head hit the back of her throat. She repressed the urge to gag. He grunted, and she whined, he jerked and pulsed against her tongue. He didn't thrust or force her, he let her have control, and it made her need him more.

Her hands came up to cup the cheeks of his ass, the hair teased her palms and the pads of her fingers. She bobbed along his thickness.

He cursed and groaned, praised her as he massaged her scalp, guiding her but never attempting to control her. A sense of power she'd never felt before caused her to increase her suction, taking him deeper on every thrust. Without thinking about it, she brought her right hand to her mouth, slipped two fingers in beside his cock, and then removed them, reaching back. She massaged around the tight muscle of her hole. Felt the resistance and flex. She hadn't finger fucked herself before, but with Gideon's dick in her mouth, her ass felt empty.

They hadn't gone beyond mutual masturbation, he didn't ask for blowjobs and didn't touch her hole. His restraint caused her to want to break him. Prove she could make him lose control. Her hand still on his ass stroked over his skin, her fingers dipped into his crease. She teased the wrinkled skin, and the salty, musk of his pre-cum grew stronger on her tongue. She withdrew until she strongly suckled the head, and flicked her tongue against the sensitive spot on the underside.

His upper body curved over hers and for a split second she froze, waited for his touch to replace hers. Then she was pushed away, she almost cried until she was forcibly lifted to her feet and spun. Her cheek met the bathroom door, and Gideon had his face buried between her ass cheeks. He ate her ass with rough nips, sucks, and prods of his tongue. His large hands kneaded and pulled until he opened her wider.

She clawed at the door. The wet, suckling sounds and grunts that vibrated against her made her sweat, her body flushed with an arousal she hadn't ever felt. Her penis was firm and aching. There wasn't a time in her past where she embraced her sexual needs. Masturbation for tension release and nothing else. Right then, she wanted sex, wanted fucking for fucking's sake. To be selfish and orgasm, feel Gideon pounding away behind her. Feel the pinch and pressure as he used her—loved her.

Her eyes rolled back as she moved her arms behind her and shoved her fingers into Gideon's soft hair. She arched her back and lifted onto her toes. She needed him closer. A guttural moan pushed passed her tight throat, and she yelped as a huge hand smack her ass, one cheek then the other.

She whimpered as he pulled away, she was about to tell him no, but he turned her around. The pleasure/pain of him drawing her into his mouth threatened to cause her knees to give out. She looked down at him, his swollen lips were wrapped around her, and he sucked, she ground against his mouth. Panic mixed with ecstasy, too much and not enough, she wanted more.

It wasn't something she'd asked for in the past, and she didn't know how to tell him.

Luckily, she didn't have too, he surged to his feet and picked her up in the process. His mouth pushed to hers, and he carried her toward the bedroom. He laid her on the bed, and she twined her arms around his neck, his tongue thrusting into her mouth. Retreating to suck and bite at her lips. She chased his mouth, felt his smile and traced it with her tongue.

She held on as he leaned to the side, she heard a drawer open, but she couldn't take her gaze off his flushed, sweaty face. He was so handsome, and he was all hers. She didn't want whatever they had to end. He encouraged her. Made her feel beautiful and sexy, things she hadn't thought in relation to herself.

She let out the most non-sexiest squeak of her life when Gideon flipped them and put her on top.

"What are you doing," she asked.

"You're in control." He pressed a bottle of lube and a condom into her hands. "Want to watch you."

She trembled and scooted down to straddle his thighs. His cock was thick and red, flushed and leaking. His thighs shook as she stroked him from base to tip, stroked her palm over the head, and back down. She opened the condom with shaking hands, almost dropping it. She finally removed it from the foil and rolled it slowly down his dick.

She gently lubed him, added more to her fingers, and brought her fingers to her hole. Two fingers easily slipped in, she shuddered and added more.

"Look at me," he ordered.

She opened her eyes and met his, they were heavy-lidded, and his breathing was ragged. She couldn't wait, she lifted onto her knees and moved up his body, she held him and held her breath. She anticipated pain, but it was nothing but pleasure as she lowered onto his cock. The pinch and burn perfection, her body shook so much, and she gripped his sides with her knees.

It was overwhelming, panic set in, and then Gideon was there. He embraced her, pulled her to him, and his mouth pressed to hers.

"Easy, baby, this is you and me. So fucking right." He groaned, kissed her between whispered words.

"Gideon."

"No matter what, you have the right to say no."

She believed him. It was there in his touch, kisses, and in his words, he'd wouldn't ever make her do anything. Even now, with him buried inside her, if she said no, he'd end it. She started to move, it was a slow, gentle rhythm. Their bodies coming together in perfect sync. They shared trembling kisses, held each other tight and when her movements faltered, he guided her with tender hands on her hips.

She grew lightheaded, she whined and moaned, begging him. The end was so close, all she needed was something more.

He braced his forearm against her ass and tugged her forward, she rubbed against the lower, hairy curve of his belly. She screamed as he suddenly lifted her from him and place her on her hands and knees. His big body blanketed hers, and she broke him, he took her in one powerful thrust. He rode her rough, he palmed her length and massaged the firmness of her flesh, stroked her in the circle of his thumb and index finger.

Skin slapped against skin, their sweaty bodies slid together, and his teeth nipped at her earlobe.

"Tell me what you want," he grunted.

"You, please, I need—"

She arched, and the angle of his thrusts changed, the force of them increased. She barely locked her legs before she squeezed her thighs shut and rolled her hips, meeting him move for move. She came with a scream that ripped her throat raw. Gideon plastered himself to her back, and the pulse of his cock and his deep groans melded perfectly with hers. Blood rushed in her ears, and she collapsed to the bed taking Gideon with her.

Her eyes widened as she realized Gideon was talking, whispering to her he loved her. His touches and kisses were gentle as he soothed her. He loved—loud clapping come from outside. Cheering like you'd heard at some sport's event.

"What the hell," Gideon jerked open the curtain.

She lifted her head to find the whole Brawlers Crew including Tank, Elijah, and Scary outside, Twitch, Hunter, and Gregory held up signs scrawled with 10s. They were all smiling as they stared toward the window.

"Oh hell, they didn't."

Gideon closed the curtain, and she looked at him like he was crazy as he started laughing like a maniac.

"I think they're louder than Psycho and Ben, damn, good one, Ghost," Twitch squealed.

"Can we get new friends," she asked.

"I don't think that's going to work, they'll hunt us down." He rolled to his back.

She smiled through her embarrassment when he pulled her across his chest.

"Say it again."

"Say what?"

"You know, please." She couldn't bring herself to look at him.

He placed his huge hand on her cheek, his thumb pushed her chin up. "You never have to beg me to say it. I was going to wait until you were—"

"Say it, Gideon."

"I love you."

She didn't wait for him to finish the words before she pressed her mouth to his, her own I love you muffled against his lips. She was happy, this was her life now. Gideon and the farm, being safe and confident. It couldn't get much better than that.

20 There Was Only One Outcome

Harper needed a distraction and what better one than practice with The Executioners. He and Harper were ready to go home, but Bull talked them into staying a few more days just to give Linus and his team a bit more time to work. They'd never be famous, and none of them wanted to be, it was their way of unwinding after rough weeks or to relax and play at Brawlers.

Most of his experience came from playing piano or guitar at weddings. His mother had insisted that he had to play an instrument when he was a kid. He'd always considered it somewhat of a chore until the first time Harper watched him. But as with all practices, they tended to end with them just hanging out. Joker had his chair leaned back, propped against the wall, with Killer happy in his hoodie pocket.

No one gave them a second look because Joker growled at anyone who looked at Killer sideways. He'd only half agreed that giving Joker something of his own was a good idea, but he hadn't realized how much Joker would get attached to the micro-puppy.

Harper nudged his ribs, and he glanced down at her to find her watching Joker.

He loved his group of friends. They were all different from each other.

Sin and Saint, blond and beautiful, rumors were they'd tried to have a modeling career in their teens. It hadn't worked out for them. Now they co-managed the local sex shop. They loved it. Their fascination with Pelter was worrisome, to say the least.

King had his no-strings-attached attitude, but he'd always thought it was King's cover. He was the lead singer and guitarist, they even said he could've made it out of Powers on his talent. King was a big guy, but strangely vulnerable. With small towns, gossip was akin to big business, and King still lived in the shadow of his high school ways.

When he'd moved there, he hadn't imagined finding a group of friends like the one he had. He didn't have to be on and pretend he enjoyed the fast pace or parties. He could go to Brawlers for a beer. His ink in the last few tears expanded to sleeves, and he loved the new him.

But the best thing was Harper. Finding someone all his own after everything with Joe ended. He had lived as a hermit except for the Crews. Getting to wake up beside her. See her smile when he came into a room.

He caught Harper's yawn. She'd gotten so used to his schedule she was up with him a six every morning and to bed early. He was making so many plans but hadn't shared them with her yet. The newness of it all caused him to be wary of asking for too much.

"Guys, we're out of here."

"Yeah, Lincoln took Mal to the movies, they should be back any minute."

King seemed to grimace at the mention of Lincoln. He felt sorry for the man, but King couldn't or wouldn't take a chance.

"We've got inventory in the morning." Sin sounded disgusted.

As usual, Saint didn't say much, he was the shyer of the two. He also seemed haunted, when Saint thought no one was looking there was a sadness to the young man.

"I'll walk out with y'all," Joker said, as he held a big hand to Killer and rocked the chair forward.

They said their goodbyes, Joker stayed behind and said he'd be out in a minute. It was still humid at midnight, the day hot as hell.

"When can we go home," Harper whispered.

"Just a little longer, Linus and his team will take care of everything."

"I know, but I miss the house."

He leaned down and brushed a kiss to her forehead. "Why don't we go home for the weekend?"

"Really?"

He was about to answer as pain exploded in his back. Harper screamed and rage burned through him as he heard the hollow sound of her body falling against the side of his truck. His legs collapsed beneath him and he took Harper with him, his body shielded hers. He felt the warmth of blood soaking his shirt.

The shadow of a man in all black loomed over them. Slurs and curses filled the night, a gun aimed passed him at Harper, then Joker tackled their attacker. The stranger fired wildly as he hit the ground with a thud. The sound of a fist connecting with flesh, the shattering of bone, and blood sprayed across his face. In the porch lights, he saw the deadness in Joker's eyes.

The attacker tried to fight back, but when that didn't work the stranger, he knew it was Bill, struggled and aimed once more. He grabbed Harper's arm and jerked her behind him, even as he tried to reach Joker. Joker and Bill fought over the weapon, both men jerked as another shot rang out.

He ignored the sirens and the crunch of gravel as he lunged toward Joker. His friend rolled to his back, and he searched Joker's blood covered chest. He barely registered in his peripheral that Sin and Saint rushed Harper into the house. King was running toward them, his phone still in his hand.

"Is he hit?"

Joker's eyes were empty, and he was deathly still, but he wasn't hurt. He turned toward Bill as the man coughed and gurgled, his hands covered a hole in his black shirt.

"No, no, but he isn't here right now."

Killer was whining and licking Joker's face, her tiny body vibrated.

Chaos suddenly reigned as paramedics and Deputies converged, they worked frantically over Bill.

He was pushed out of the way as another paramedic checked out Joker. He'd never seen Joker that pale. His body stiff and his breathing was too shallow.

He struggled to his feet, his gaze darted toward the house, and he smiled at Harper, attempted to reassure her. Then adrenaline quickly disappeared, and agony took him down. He heard Harper scream his name. The voices and movements around him were panicked, his shirt was pushed up. King called for help, and it was the last thing he heard.

He awoke slowly to the annoying beeps of monitors and a low drone of voices. The scent of antiseptic and Harper teased his senses. He forced his eyes open and turned his head to find Harper sobbing.

"Hey, baby, don't do that," he soothed as his voice cracked.

"Gideon," her voice quiet and filled with anguish.

"What the hell happened?"

"Bill shot you. They said...said you probably didn't realize until—"

That's when it all came rushing back. The attack. Joker's seeming catatonic state. Bill probably dying.

"Shit, are you okay, he didn't?" He tried to turn and search her for even the smallest bruise, but realized his mistake as his wound pulled.

"Gideon, stop, I'm fine."

"You fucking do that shit to me again, Gideon Jane, I will kill you my damn self."

He groaned at Carol's pissed off voice. How long had he been out?

"Carol, don't start."

"Don't start, don't start, who the fuck you think you're talking to?"

"Ma'am, you really need to calm down or—"

A male nurse tried but failed to calm Carol down. He suddenly felt sorry for the young man. Carol's fists were rested on the ample flare of her hips. Her skin-tight dress looked like she'd walked out of a club minutes before. He swore the man was barely keeping his eyes off the obscene cleavage right in his face. Man, how he loved his oldest friend.

"You tell me to calm down one more time, boy, you won't like what I do."

"She's threatened to spank him several times," Harper whispered in his ear.

"She likes him."

"Really?"

He let out a weak chuckle at the look on Harper's face.

"Bill?"

"He died on route to the hospital."

"What about Joker?"

"Not good, he had a flashback. As soon as he came around, he checked himself out against doctor's orders. Pelter took him home."

"What's going to happen to him?"

"With what happened, it's being ruled self-defense. Pelter's not going to pursue it. Joker disappeared off the grid, he's out at the old shack."

The shack was exactly how it sounded. A falling down four walls in the middle of nowhere. Only way in was a long ass hike.

"Anybody go and check on him?"

"Sin and Saint did a flyover in their Cessna. They caught sight of Joker chopping wood. It was proof of life, so they didn't try to land and hike in."

Probably for the best, Joker had to work out his own issues. After all the touching and prodding, Joker's temper and nerves were probably raw. He'd only seen Joker lose it once in the years he'd known him. Last time, it had been simply someone coming up behind him and rapping him on the shoulder. Joker had spun and narrowly stopped himself from punching an elderly man who needed help.

They said Joker was crazy, but to survive the situation Joker had and come out even partially functioning was a miracle.

"Gideon, I'm sorry, if you don't want…if I'm too much trouble…"

"I love you, baby, don't think any different. What happened doesn't change that. We'll go home to our house. We'll plan our future, and this will all be a bad memory. Got me?"

She nodded, and her lip trembled, so he tugged her closer and kissed her. Tasted the salt of her tears. Sensed when some of her dread drained from her. He knew Bill would be a problem. It hadn't changed the fact he'd wanted her and always would. They couldn't guarantee that tomorrow would come, but he wouldn't give her up for anything.

"Love you," she whispered against his mouth.

He smiled as he deepened the kiss and couldn't wait to see what tomorrow would bring with his Harper.

Epilogue: Having a Prince Charming Wasn't so Bad

Harper finished up setting the table and waited for Gideon to come inside. The windows were repaired on the house and greenhouse, the siding replaced where a few stray bullets had hit. Everything was back to normal, well, her new normal, and she loved it. She had moved all her things into their room. *Their room.* She still couldn't get over it.

Best part of her day, though, was waiting for him to come home. She didn't know why, but she loved walking around their house or lounging on the couch naked. She loved her new confidence. The way she was finally happy and healthy. She wouldn't say she didn't have her bad days, they both did, although, they were few and farther between.

They talked about the future, and she understood they were still new, it had only been four months since they'd gotten together. A lot had happened. The biggest change was being free of Bill. She no longer had to look over her shoulder. She didn't have to worry about being hurt or humiliated. Gideon treated her as if she were the best thing in his life and he made her feel that way. That she was perfect as is and loved. She'd worked through her doubts, the lingering fear and panic. She felt free.

Gideon hadn't tried to change her, and because of that, she'd found herself. She was even looking into buying Nightingale's because Clora wanted to retire. She had a home. A prospective business. And a man who loved her— not what she let the world see.

It was quick, but it felt right, she didn't want to think about a future without him.

She checked the time and rushed for the door with Tiny right on her heels. She pushed open the screen door just in time to watch Gideon walk across the yard. He was all healed from the gunshot. He'd almost lost a kidney, but he'd been lucky. Bill had been drunk the night of the attack, and his aim hadn't been true.

A smile curved his mouth as he jogged up the steps, swinging her into his arms.

"I was wondering if you were coming in anytime soon."

"I had to check the shipment of orchids you wanted. Did you miss me?"

"Of course, and also, I'm hungry, I've been waiting on dinner."

"Let me wash up, and we'll eat."

He set her on her feet, and she bent over to pick Tiny up, then they headed into the house. The screen door banged behind them. She glanced behind her to find him watching the sway of her hips, the gentle bounce of her ass, and she almost forgot she was hungry.

Gideon always seemed to want her. She'd lost count of the times over the last month that he'd awakened her, his touch gentle, and he told her he loved her at every opportunity. She would never grow tired of hearing it.

He washed his hands and took a seat at the already set table. She sat down on his right. Twitch had sent home several casseroles when they'd returned to the farm. She wasn't much of a cook. She wouldn't give anyone food poisoning, but gourmet she wasn't. It was a good thing her man was happy with simple food—steaks and veggies she could do.

"Harper, there's something I wanted to ask you."

She became nervous at the hesitancy in his tone.

"What?"

"Have you ever thought of having kids?"

She lowered her head, placed her fork on her plate and folded her hands in her lap. They hadn't discussed kids before. Sometimes she thought he avoided the conversation, even though neither of them brought it up.

"It's okay, forget I asked."

He tried to change the subject, and she didn't like the hurt in his tone.

"I always wanted kids. Have you ever thought about it?"

It would be too much to dream about, him, kids, a home, and it was all too much. The pessimistic side of her still waited for the bottom to drop out or she'd wake up from their perfect dream, and be right back where she was.

"I'll answer if you look at me, baby."

She took a deep breath and lifted her chin, but it took her a minute to meet his gaze.

"Do you want babies with me?"

"That's a question, not an answer, Gideon."

"Well, it pertains to the answer."

"I don't want to answer wrong."

"There's no wrong or right answer, Harper, this is just you and me. We've discussed our future, what we want, but this is one topic we haven't brought up."

"I want babies, or I'd settle for a baby with you."

"Then when the time is right we'll decide on adoption or surrogacy. Whatever works for us."

She jumped from her chair and threw her arms around him. She couldn't contain the tears.

"But do you know what we have to do first?" He gently tugged her head back.

"What's that? The house is great. We both work. It a safe place, we'd be great—"

She closed her mouth so fast her teeth clicked as a small black box appeared in front of her. That couldn't be—she started to get up, but Gideon's hold on her tightened.

"I know, when we've talked, we've established we're in this all the way, but you've never said you wanted to get married. Maybe you didn't think about it, but I did. I want forever, marriage, and kids if we decide on the right time. Harper, I love you, will you marry me?"

She didn't know what to say, she was frozen, and when he opened the box, she started to shake. He wanted to marry her, have kids, it was everything she'd wanted and refused to hope for, and now it was all right there. Revealed within the facets of stone, shimmered in white gold, and shined in his blue-green eyes. She pushed her mouth to his, nodded, as she felt his smile. The almost suffocating embrace she held him in.

It was perfect, for someone who hadn't dreamed of a happily ever after all her own…it was everything. Who knew when she was eleven and swore she'd have a Prince Charming that at almost thirty, she'd find him and it wasn't so bad.

THE END

About the Author

By day, J.M. is an introverted cook hiding out in her kitchen in the middle of nowhere Ohio, by night and any free time she may have, she is a writer of mainly LGBTQ Fiction and Erotica. Although. she's equal opportunity when it comes to telling a story, she'll even write a bit of straight erotic romance when the mood strikes.

She has been writing for years in old notebooks. At the age of eight, she wrote the worst poem in the history of poetry, but it sparked her love for writing. She reads too much and loves to get lost in other worlds and her favorite stories have to include laughter and having the reader doing at least one double take. Thirty-something, forever restless she uses her stories to ground herself, and find her place of peace.

WHERE TO FIND J.M.
www.jmdabneyauthor.com